ARNETTA AND THE
MiRROR OF DeSTiNY

If HOME is where the heart is,
I hope Arnetta finds her
way into yours!
Jeannie Chambers

JEANNIE CHAMBERS

RED PRESS CO.

Red Press Co., Inc.

published@redpressco.com

Publisher's Note: This is a work of fiction. Names, characters, places, and incidents are a product of the author's imagination. Locales and public names are sometimes used for atmospheric purposes. Any resemblance to actual people, living or dead, or to businesses, companies, events, institutions, or locales is completely coincidental.

Ordering Information: Special discounts are available on quantity purchases by corporations, associations, and others. For details, contact the publisher at the address above.

First Edition

PRINTED IN THE USA

ISBN 978-1-7333559-5-7

LCCN 2020944945

For you, my reader.
I hope you find home wherever you are.

The ache for home lives in all of us. - Mya Angelou

ACKNOWLEDGMENTS

I'd like to thank the people of Landreth, a fictitious textile mill town in upstate SC. I enjoyed stepping back in time to 1985 and meeting some of your residents.

A special shout out to my street team, Jeannie and the Liwits! You guys are amazing, and I appreciate all your comments and helping spread the word about Arnetta's story.

Many thanks to my good friends, old and new. Marie, I still have the framed poem you gave me of one of my early writing days. To members of the Highlands Writer's group, who are constantly encouraging me and my writing. Bud, I always feel blessed to be a part of 'the best two hours' on Tuesday.

As always, my publisher, Red Press Co.'s Monica Collier for your support and everything you do to get my books in the hands of readers.

To my family, especially Susan and Erin for always believing in me, and Tucker for the idea to use one of my grandchildren as Arnetta for marketing, Lydia, you rocked it! XOXOXO. And of course, to my earthly father, Ira Skelton. I'd like to think he's looking down on me with a smile, knowing that Arnetta's story started with the mirror he gave me years ago. I'm blessed beyond measure, and give credit to my heavenly father for everything.

1

The Mirror

There were no survivors. Arnetta had that feeling. That feeling she always got when this kind of storm was brewing. The reality of the crash still flashed through her mind during thunderstorms. Walking, almost running on the Collier Street sidewalk, head lowered to avoid the giant raindrops as she tried to miss the occasional puddle in the uneven pavement. *I'm going to be soaked to the skin if I don't find somewhere...anywhere.* Her waist-length, strawberry-blonde hair stuck to her back as if it were trying to duck for cover. *If only I could be so lucky.* She raised her head enough to notice the OPEN sign of the What's New Shop and darted underneath the awning and opened the door just as a menacing clap of thunder split open the sky. A bell jingled as she entered, but all she heard was the dead quiet. Well, that and the pounding beat of her heart in her ears. *There were no survivors.* The hair standing on the back of her neck like sentry guards, her throat felt like it had a golf ball inside. *It's just a storm, Arnetta. Only a storm. Gosh, it's dark in here. Wait, what's that?* Straining to hear the static sound coming from a radio somewhere, she recognized the voice as the NPR man giving the hourly national news. Arnetta listened while her eyes searched the dark store for signs of life.

"Last Sunday, January 20, 1985, history was made. At age 73, President Reagan is now the oldest President to ever lead this country."

Seventy-three does seem awfully old, but he doesn't really look any older than some of the other presidents in my eleventh-grade U.S. History book.

Arnetta passed by this antique store almost every day but had never gone inside. Today probably wouldn't have been any different if she hadn't forgotten her raincoat at the dentist's office and wasn't deathly afraid of thunderstorms. She turned around and looked outside at the downpour through her fogged lenses. *I hate wearing glasses. I wish these had windshield wipers; somebody could make a fortune if only...* The heavy drops were like guided missiles exploding on the sidewalk. She removed her glasses to try and wipe them clear using a dry spot at the hem of her nearly soaked shirt.

A distant voice called out, "Can I help you find something?"

Arnetta jerked her head upward and squinted her eyes to better focus in the direction of the unknown voice. "Um, no Ma'am, I'm just looking, thanks." She put on her glasses and spotted the source of the voice and realized it had come from a man. A little man. "Oh, sorry, no Sir." He was sitting beside an old roll-top desk. The top was open, exposing papers jutting out from most of the little cubbyholes. He wore round, black-framed glasses way down on his nose so that when he talked, his eyes had to reach high, raising his bushy eyebrows. His graying hair was so thin there seemed to be only a few strands combed over the top of his balding head. *He looks like an owl, an old owl.*

"I bet you're glad I'm open today." The little man said as he turned off the radio and then sort of scooted off his perch and waddled towards her. "That's one big storm out there, isn't it? The power went out just as you entered with that big boom."

"But...the radio."

"Batteries kicked in; besides, I usually don't have it on when customers are in the store."

Arnetta eyed the little man. He *was* a little man, a very tiny man. *Great. Now he thinks I'm a customer.* She had never considered herself either tall or short at five-foot-four-inches, but she had never, in all of her almost sixteen years, been face to face with a full-grown man that was shorter than she was, and this man was at least a foot shorter than she was. She was still standing within three feet of the entrance. Her stomach was still in a knot from the storm and now more feelings of dread entered in the mix. *I think I'm going to be sick.* She looked back outside at the gloomy mess of a day and then turned back toward him. *It's better in here than out there. I'm sure it's OK. Creepy, but OK.*

"Yes, Sir, I am glad you're open, that's an awful storm. Hey, I've never been in here before. I can't see much, but there sure looks like there's a lot of stuff in here. Where'd it all come from?" *I've had these jitters plenty of times before. I'm just here to pass the storm.* Arnetta took a step closer, the same way she would approach an unknown dog. "The name says What's New, so I figured there'd be new stuff in here."

"It's all relative."

Arnetta cocked her head with a big question mark on her face.

"Relative." He paused, while looking out towards the rows of eclectic furnishings, then continued, "Relative to how you perceive, or use the word new. The first thing most returning customers to any antique or consignment store want to know is, what's new, as in, are there any new items in your store since I was here last? Anyway, that's how the store got its name."

Arnetta answered with a quick smile while glancing at items within view behind the little man. The light provided by subdued daylight through the store's floor-to-ceiling glass windows seemed a little brighter, or maybe her eyes were just adjusting. She slid her backpack off one shoulder with a shrug and guided it to the floor using her other arm. *This thing is so bulky, I don't want to break anything.* She advanced a couple of steps, leaving her belongings by the door.

"What's that?" she asked as she pointed to a small tan-colored thing on top of a little vanity.

His eyes followed hers as he waddled over about three steps and placed his hand the selected piece, picked it up and said, "This?"

"Yes, it looks like a fancy ping-pong paddle or something, but there's only one. What is it?"

He brought it over towards Arnetta. *There's that waddle again. I wonder if one of his legs shorter than the other.* When he got right in front of her, he flipped it over so she could look at it closer.

"Oh, it's a mirror, how beautiful! How old is this thing?" One side was a mirror, and the backside had an intricate design on it. It was very old looking because the grooves of the design had what looked like years of caked dust in it, but the design itself was easy to see. It looked like a faerie princess in a long billowing dress, and her hair seemed to flow the length of the gown. *It appears like she's looking back as she's running, while holding her dress up in front to keep from stumbling.* She was running away from something. Or, maybe she was running towards something and was looking back as if beckoning someone to follow. Arnetta could barely take her eyes off the winsome figure. She traced the design with her index finger while he held it. "May I hold it?"

"Yes, but be very careful, this mirror is an antique, I'm guessing late eighteenth century."

"Sure. OK." She said as she took the mirror with both hands.

"A lot of work went into this one. Hand carved maple. Looks like someone had painted it white at one time. I've never seen another one like it. It came from an old abandoned cabin found by a lady that had just bought a large parcel of land near here. I got quite a few things from her; you may be interested in..."

"How much does a thing like this cost? My Gummy would love this I bet." Arnetta was mesmerized with the carving.

"Gummy?"

"Yeah, oh, Gummy is my grandmother. When my older brother, James was little, he couldn't say granny, so gummy is what came out, and that's the name that stuck. Arnetta started to return the mirror to the vanity face down like it was, but then remembered something. *I never got to see my teeth after the dentist.* She held the mirror and stretched out her arm toward the street, but she couldn't see much because the store was darker than the dim light from the still-darkened skies. All she got was a silhouette. She turned around, so the light from outside would be at her back and held the mirror up again. *Now, that's better.* She smiled big showing the reflection of her newly cleaned teeth. *Hmmph. I never really can tell a difference, but they sure feel...*

"Oh, my gosh! Did you see that?" Arnetta screeched as she whirled around to get a better look outside.

"What? See What?" The man carefully pried the mirror from Arnetta's clutch and then craned his neck to get a better look himself.

"A wreck. I saw a wreck. In the mirror. I could see it happening, but..." Arnetta had that feeling again, down deep in the pit of her stomach like she was going to be sick.

The shop keeper placed the mirror back on top of the vanity and followed Arnetta as she ran to the door, jerked it open, and stood underneath the awning. He joined her as they both stared into the street and then to each other. He had a strange look on his face when he said, "I don't see anything. Maybe it was just the light playing tricks on your eyes. Sometimes the reflection of the sun on cars out here will just about blind me for a minute or two."

"No. I know what I saw. I didn't hear anything, but I know what I saw! Besides, there is no sun shining. It was an old blue car." Arnetta pointed to the curb, "It was right here in front of your store! It ran into the parking meter and knocked it over, and there was a girl..."

They continued to stand there. The rain had stopped, but the threat of more could be seen in the low dark clouds. The little man quietly said, "The parking meters are all still there, there is no blue car, and there is no girl. I think you should come back inside and sit a spell." He gently touched her elbow to guide her as if she were blind, "Come, and let's get in out of this damp air. I've got a Coca-Cola in the drink box. I want to hear more about what you think you saw, if you're up to it."

2

Little Man

The man guided Arnetta to an upholstered armchair near his roll-top desk. She sat down, folded her arms in front of her, and watched her legs involuntarily shake up and down. Arnetta had balled her fists, a bad habit she's had as long as she could remember. That habit forced her to keep her fingernails short; otherwise she'd leave marks in the palm of her hands, and sometimes they bled. Not a pretty picture and hard to explain. It was mostly an unnoticeable habit and seemed to give her an edge as if she would be ready for anything. She used to pretend when she was eight years old, as she clenched her fists until her palms were indented, that it gave her superpowers. While she waited for the man to return with her Coke, the lights came on and she began to feel more at ease. *That man must think I'm crazy. Obviously, I couldn't have seen what I thought I saw.* She decided when he came back, she'd just tell him he was right. *It had been a reflection or something. I mean, it had to be, right?* Arnetta noticed her legs had stopped shaking. *OK. I'm OK.*

As she looked around, she realized she'd only seen a tiny bit of the store. It seemed to go on forever with row after row of old furniture and doodads. There was a tall, skinny wooden chest of drawers that had each of the twelve drawers partially opened with old crocheted things hanging out of them. There was an old squatty vanity shaped sort of like a lima bean with a big round cushioned seat pushed into the curve. It had an enormous unframed oval mirror attached. She imagined some old lady sitting there, then realized it probably wasn't some old lady, it may have belonged to a younger person, but it would've been a very long time ago. She imagined a girl her age sitting there brushing her hair. She stood and walked the few steps to the vanity and although it was jammed next to other furniture, she was able to pull out the velvet covered seat and sit down in front of the mirror. *Wow. This reminds me of that painting in my art class of a girl looking at her reflection in a dirty window. I've never seen a mirror like this one. I know it must be ancient because the edges are all blackened.* Her hand instinctively went to the border to see if she could somehow rub the black off. The glass was thick and cold, but smooth on the front and back.

"The silver's coming off of that one."

Arnetta jumped and turned around to see the little man's hand holding the offered Coke. *Geez! Scare me to death why dontcha! There's that creepy feeling again.* Go away, she told her inner feelings while trying to form a smile.

Arnetta took a long swallow from the bottle of Coke, then asked, "What do you mean? About the silver coming off?"

He stepped closer and reached up to a part of the mirror that had a black spot about the size of a quarter. "See this?"

What she saw was an old little hand, with a big gold ring on it. The ring had a filigree initial with a little diamond chip in it. The initial was 'M'.

"Pretty ring. What's the initial stand for?"

"One question at a time. And by the way, I'm glad to see you've had a chance to calm down a little."

"Thanks for the Coke, it's just been a weird day. I d-don't like storms much, I guess I just got over excited. I have an overactive imagination sometimes." She pointed to his ring. "Is that your initial, or is it just a ring you are selling in your store?"

"Questions, questions. First, you'd asked about the silver." He tapped the edge of the mirror and continued, "When I say the silver is coming off this mirror, what I mean is the backing has started to erode. Do you know what separates a mirror from an ordinary piece of glass?"

"No sir." Arnetta glanced down at her Lucite Mickey Mouse watch. *I sure don't want a science lesson right now either.*

As if he could read her thoughts, he added, "Well, that's not a bad thing. Most people never give it a second thought. Without going into the whole process, I'll just say this, you take a piece of glass and paint the back with a metal that will reflect. Back when this mirror was made, they were still using mercury mixed with silver or tin; it's called amalgam. Now they use mostly aluminum, I think. Have you ever had a tooth filled at the dentist? That's amalgam too."

"Ewww. I just left Dr. Wilmer's office down the street. That's where my raincoat is." Arnetta looked outside through the store windows. The clouds had lifted. *I've got to get going.* She looked at her Coca-Cola. *I'll leave after I finish my drink.* She continued with her thought process. "I guess I never thought about what was in a filling. I wonder why they don't fill your teeth with something that's the same color of your teeth?"

"I think they do when they can, but the amalgam holds up better. Although something just came out in the paper the other day of a new study that said the mercury in the amalgam fillings may be dangerous because a small part of it could travel to your brain. Who knows?" The little man turned back to the mirror. "I never suggest people change these old mirrors. If you want to see a less distorted image, get a new mirror." He touched the black speckled mirror like it was fragile and said, "Best to keep these old mirrors just like they are. No telling what images they may have seen, you go to messing with the back of them to repair them, and those old images may just rub off on you."

Arnetta stared at him with wide eyes, but then she saw a grin sneak across his face traveling all the way to his eyes. Those eyes looked bulging and creepy behind his magnifying lenses, but she began to realize he wasn't so weird after all. He'd managed to get her mind off the accident she'd seen outside, and he hadn't brought it up even though he'd said he wanted her to tell him about it. *Sneaky, possibly, but not creepy.* Her eyes locked in on his ring again. She answered him with a "Hardy-Har-Har. I knew you were joking. Hey, that is a nice ring. Is it from this store? Is it old?"

"No and yes. My mother gave me this signet ring when I graduated from college."

"What does the M stand for?"

"It's my initials. M stand for Mann, my last name. That's M-A-N-N" He spelled out the name as he balled his fist and brought the initialed ring closer to Arnetta's face, "and see the little diamond? See what's next to it?"

Arnetta looked. She didn't see anything at first but looking closer she saw what looked like a teeny curvy line, sort of a curlicue design. "Yeah, what is it?"

"Well, that's a capital L, albeit small, and that's the meaning."

"Meaning of what?"

"Meaning of my initial ring and my initials. Big M and a little L."

Arnetta looked at him, and feeling a little dumb, said, "I don't get it."

"Well, in case you haven't noticed, and I'm sure you have, you're just being nice, which is a sign of a good up-bringing I might add, but just in case you haven't noticed, I'm not particularly of normal height." He used two fingers of each hand to make air quotes when he said the word normal. "I loved my mother, but I don't know what she was thinking when she named me. My initials are L.M. which stand for Little Mann, and that's my name.

"Oh my gosh!" Arnetta squealed without considering of how that would make him feel, but he just shrugged one of his shoulders a fraction and grinned, "So your real name, it's Little Mann?"

He removed a pretend hat and bowed low as he said, "Little Mann at your service."

She couldn't help but to smile, and replied with a head nod, "Pleased to meet you Mr. Little Mann," she nodded in return, "My name is Arnetta Price."

3

Arnetta

Y ou can call me L.M. if you'd like. That's what most people call me. It usually comes out sounding something like Ale Lim around these parts, but that's OK too. You can call me anything but midget and late for dinner." He said the last part with a little laugh, but Arnetta had the feeling he was serious about the M-word.

Arnetta made her way down one aisle and crossed over to the next one. Little Mann stayed back by the vanity. Occasionally, she would reach out and touch an item or pick it up to examine it a little closer. When she'd gotten back near where Little Mann was standing, she turned to him and spoke over a display of old books on a chest-high shelf.

"I didn't mean to laugh at your name. It's just that, well, can I ask you a personal question?"

"Why, certainly, Arnetta."

"Well, I guess it's just that both our mothers had a weird sense of humor when they were naming us, but.... how did your mama know? I mean, how did she know you'd be a little man when you were born?"

"Good question, Arnetta. The doctor diagnosed it, but sometimes they can't even tell when a baby will be different. Things have changed by now, I'm sure, but back then they told my mama it was probably because my dad had been too old to have children. Can you believe that? Why in the Bible, I think Abraham was about 75 years old when he had a child, now *that's* old. My father was 50 years old when I was born, but I've met plenty of people older than that who have fathered children with no adverse effects. I don't know what happened, but it happened, and here I am, living proof that little people can grow to a ripe old age. L.M. straightened up a few items on the aisle he was on, while continuing, "You said your mother had a good sense of humor when she named you? What do you mean? I think Arnetta is a beautiful name."

"Thanks. It's just that there's no one else in school with a name like mine. Everybody tells me it sounds like an old lady name. Some of the boys call me 'Are Notta.' It's so embarrassing sometimes. Teachers mispronounce it too, sometimes they call me Anita. That's how 'Are Notta' got started. A boy, trying to make a play on words, corrected the teacher with "No Ma'am, it are not Anita, her name is Arnetta," the teacher only heard the first part and called me Arnotta for days."

"Well, I could sure tell you about being made fun of, and not just my name. How did you get the name Arnetta?

Arnetta dropped her shoulders like she'd done so many times before when she explained her name. She often wondered how her mama and daddy ever got together in the first place, they didn't even share the same tastes. *Here goes. One more time. Thanks, Mama.*

"You ever hear of Gunsmoke? It was a popular western on TV when I was born."

"Sure, I used to watch it all the time. Everybody loves Matt Dillion! He was the hero that saved the Wild West every week. Well, he and those Cartwrights from Bonanza."

Arnetta rolled her eyes. *Geez.* "Yep, that's him. Do you remember the actor's name that played Matt Dillion?"

"Yes, of course, I do. James Arness, right? Oh, I see. You were named Arnetta for Arness?"

"Yes, but that's only part of it. Have you ever heard of Etta James?

"The jazz singer, Etta James? Well, of course, everybody has. Well, everybody that likes good music anyway. I'm not *that* old, but I am a few years older than Miss James. I used to listen to her on the radio- what was that song? Let me see..." He closed his eyes, and then a slight smile came across his face. Arnetta thought she saw him sway from side to side, but just a little. His eyes jumped open as he said, "That's it. At Last. That's the song, At Last. She was really something. I haven't heard anything from her lately, though."

Arnetta explained her name all the time to people, but most of the time, it was to kids her own age, and they never knew who James Arness or Etta James was. His recognition made her smile. "Well, the story goes, my mama was a big fan of Etta James, and my daddy was a bigger fan of Gunsmoke. So, there you have it: A-R-N from James Arness and E-T-T-A from Etta James.

"Could be worse." L.M. grinned.

"Yeah? How?" Arnetta had the slightest scowl on her face. She didn't like having her name being made fun of any more than L.M. detested hearing the 'M' word.

"Well, they could've named you 'Miss Kitty'" he said, as he slapped his leg and let out a laugh.

"Ha-ha. Not funny." But she couldn't help the sneaky grin that crawled up her face. Her daddy used to call her Miss Kitty all the time. She sure missed her daddy. She missed her mother too, but her daddy had been her best friend before the accident.

She noticed the inside of the store brighten up gradually as if more lights had been switched on. She looked out to see a few white puffy clouds. *This has been fun, but my time here is done.* "Well, it looks like the storm is over, and I've really got to get home."

"Well, Arnetta, it's been my pleasure to meet you and have your company this afternoon. I hope you'll come back in some time even when the wind doesn't blow you in."

Arnetta rolled her eyes and smiled as she picked up her book bag and opened the door to leave. "I will come back. Promise. It was nice meeting you too."

Arnetta turned down the sidewalk towards the dentist's office. She hoped they were still open, but Mickey Mouse on her wrist was pointing to almost five o'clock. *Oh gosh, today's Thursday. Gummy will be upset if I'm late getting home, but I've got to try.* Arnetta really didn't want to have to go back to the dentist's office on Monday just to get her raincoat, but she knew they were closed on Fridays. As soon as she rounded the corner, she knew they were closed because there were no cars in the parking lot. *Darn it.* No sense in going on, so she turned on her heels and started back, this time towards home.

4

Home

Arnetta called it home, but it really wasn't. Most of the time, she considered herself an orphan. She lived with her grandparents, Gummy and Papaw. The only people that lived with their grandparents were orphans like her or people that had horrible parents. She knew some of those people too. She'd had a good friend, Sheila, that stayed with her grandmother, Mammy, every weekend because beginning Friday at about six o'clock, her mother would be drunk, and she'd stay that way until at least Sunday evening. She'd had another friend Billy. He was two years older than her, but she'd lost touch with him. Billy had lived in foster homes. A judge and his parents decided he couldn't live at home anymore because he kept skipping school and getting into trouble. According to Billy, his parents told the judge, "No matter what we do, he won't mind, we can't take it anymore. Let somebody else have him." Arnetta wasn't sure where Billy was today because he had to go to another foster home since his first foster family wanted to raise smaller children and having a teenage boy in the house didn't fit in with their plans. Billy used to tell Arnetta he couldn't wait until his eighteenth birthday, so he could be on his own, so maybe now Billy was free.

Arnetta thought of people like herself, Sheila, and Billy as floaters. Floaters are people who float around like feathers after a pillow fight. They eventually settle down, but when and where was determined by their circumstances. She thought of the girl she'd seen in the little mirror at the What's New shop. *Who is she? Does she have a real home, or is she a floater too? That girl had the coldest, darkest eyes I've ever seen, and they were looking right into mine. There's got to be a story behind that lifeless stare.* Arnetta shook her head to erase the mental picture in her brain as if it were an Etch-a-Sketch.

Arnetta gathered her life wasn't really that bad. Not really. Not if she kept telling herself it wasn't anyway. It surely wasn't as bad as Sheila's, or Billy's and probably not as bad as mirror girl's either. It's just that everybody else at her school had parents. She wanted parents. Everybody at school complained about their parents. First, she'd give anything, only to have parents, her real parents, and secondly, she hated the fact that she didn't have the privilege of complaining about her parents. Not that she would, but it'd sure be nice to have the option. She cared deeply for her grandparents, she did, but she couldn't really call it love, as in the kind of love most people have for their grandparents. There was a constant, sort of a detached feeling. She had the idea the feeling was mutual. She had always wondered if things had been different if theirs would've been a normal relationship. If, if and if. Her grandmother had told her many times, "If, if and if don't exist. If is for fairy tales. This is life. Deal with it." *Yep, Gummy's a realist all right, never one to sugar coat anything.* Her Papaw wasn't much different, but he mostly stayed on the sidelines. He ruled the household, but he was sort of like the wizard behind the curtain. You knew the rules. You knew they were his rules, but if you broke the rules, Gummy was the enforcer.

Arnetta rounded the corner for the last stretch towards her house. She smirked as she pictured her Gummy in a suit of armor waiting at the door, with her sword ready as she crossed the threshold. She really wasn't all that bad. Gummy was about five feet tall and had a head full of curly gray hair. She and Papaw had retired from Landreth Mills not long after she'd arrived. The house they lived in was in the Landreth Mill Village. Papaw was a short little man, but at five foot six, he was nothing like L.M. *He used to seem so much taller.* All they had known was the textile mill. They worked hard but never talked about their job. Arnetta remembered the time her family had come for a visit for a long weekend and arrived early on a Friday. She and James weren't allowed to see Gummy and Papaw until after their grandparents had enough time for them to get presentable, as they'd say.

There she was, standing in the open doorway, not worried about letting any heat out. *If that was me standing there, I would have never heard the end of it.* "It's about time you came home Arnetta. I was about to send a posse out to look for you. Dentist office called over an hour ago and said you'd left your raincoat."

Arnetta walked up the steps, through the front door, and said in passing, "I'm sorry to have worried you, Gummy. I went into a store downtown to wait out the storm. Doubt the raincoat would've done me much good, in that kind of rain, but I'll get it Monday. Sorry. I'll be right back down to help with dinner after I get out of my wet clothes."

"You do that; you know your Papaw don't like to eat too late." Gummy stood by the closed door and was talking to Arnetta's back as she started up the stairs.

"Yes, Ma'am." She answered, remembering many times when an exchange with her grandmother wouldn't be as pleasant. Arnetta couldn't forget one of the first significant encounters with Gummy.

When she had started third grade, Arnetta had only been living with Gummy and Papaw for a few weeks. It was all still new, and her grandparents were trying to make the *new* family thing work. Gummy and Papaw were working their final few weeks before their early retirement.

They had a neighbor pick Arnetta up from school, bring her home, give her a snack, and turn on the TV. Homework would come later after supper.

Arnetta found out from people at school, the reason her grandparents didn't talk about their job was that they were probably ashamed to be lintheads. She found out the meaning of so many things that day. First on the dusty playground of Mount Vista Elementary School, and then later when she got home.

"Lintheads?"

"Yeah," her classmate Nancy replied, "They work in a cotton mill. They're around cotton all day inside the mill. Some of the lint flies in the air and gets in their hair and all over their clothes. It happens to everybody."

"How do you know? Do your Mama and Daddy work in the mill too?"

"No!" the perfectly dressed Nancy snipped, "Are you kidding? My mother is a high school teacher, and my Daddy works at the bank, but they told me about lintheads. They said it's nothing to be ashamed about. They said lintheads are just like me, well sort of." Nancy looked at Arnetta through her perfectly cropped black bangs and smiled as she continued, "We're all the same, and we all have to work, play and go to school together. We just don't mix."

Nancy turned on her heels and walked away, leaving Arnetta literally in the dust. Arnetta didn't have a chance to tell Nancy that her mama and daddy didn't work in the mill either. Her mama worked in a bank too, she was a teller up at the Savings & Loan, and her daddy was a mailman. She didn't get a chance to tell her new friend Nancy that her parents were the best parents even, but that didn't matter anymore. For all practical purposes, they had left her in the dust too.

Supper was always at six o'clock. Sharp. No exceptions. Well, that was the way it was B.A. That's B for before and A for Arnetta. Papaw was so set in his ways; he thought the world might just crack off its axis if dinner wasn't on the table at six. He learned differently due to science fairs at school, and later with basketball games and other school events that his stomach was a lot more tolerant that his brain had been.

That afternoon, after the Nancy lesson, Arnetta couldn't wait for Gummy to come home so she could tell her about lintheads. Since Gummy and Papaw didn't talk about their work, she figured Gummy would be proud of her for learning something on her own. That's not the way it worked out.

"Arnetta, how was school today?" the usual question that started off dinner conversation. She always had to have an answer. She'd tried the 'OK' response, but that usually ran into "Well, what did you learn?" and one thing she *had* learned was never to say *nothing* or *I don't know*. She was

31

expected to say at least one thing she learned. It didn't matter if it was something as ridiculous as the color orange, but to Gummy and Papaw, an answer was an answer.

"School was good." Arnetta plopped a big spoonful of mashed potatoes on her plate, her favorite.

"What did you learn?" Papaw was cutting his roast beef on his plate while Gummy was passing the green beans.

"I learned about lintheads."

Papaw dropped his knife and fork in his plate, breaking one of Gummy's china plates. The ones with the faded yellow roses around the rim. *Oh boy, is he ever in trouble. Gummy is looking at Papaw like she just bit her lip.* Gummy stood up fast, knocking the ladder back chair over, reached over and grabbed both sections of the broken plate and stormed over towards the back door, and slammed it in the trash can. Then she came back to the table, snatched Arnetta up by the shoulders and marched her to her bedroom. *Talk about the world coming off its axis? What's going on? I didn't break the plate!* Once she was in her room, she noticed Gummy's face was all red, and her eyes were funny. Arnetta had never seen anyone's pupils like that before, it was like a tiny black dot lost in the middle of her caramel brown eyes, like a little boat lost in a tumultuous sea of thoughts.

"Now tell me, Miss Smarty Pants. Tell me what you think you know about lintheads!"

Arnetta proceeded to tell her what she'd been told, only she left out the part about who informed her and about not mixing. When she finished, Gummy apologized for grabbing her up and held her hard and smothering close. Just when Arnetta thought she couldn't breathe another breath, Gummy let out a stifled moan, then released her grip as she wiped her eyes. Arnetta felt terrible. Even though she didn't understand the anger, she knew from that moment on that you don't always say everything you know. She also really wanted those mashed potatoes that she never got to eat. After that night, every time she saw mashed potatoes, she thought about lintheads, and never touched them again.

5

Every Day In The
Now And Then

E ven though late, Arnetta reached the house just in
time to help with supper. Gummy was fixing breakfast for supper, which meant pancakes with peanut butter
(Papaw's favorite), eggs, bacon, grits, biscuits and gravy,
and some kind of fruit. There was a little chill in the air
after the rainstorm, but nothing like January should be.
Arnetta hadn't worn a coat all week. It had turned cold after the rainstorm. The weatherman on TV said we were
going to be in for some very cold weather. Papaw always
said eating breakfast for supper was the best thing to chase
a chill away, of course, that may have been his excuse for
requesting breakfast in the evening. Their usual breakfast
was either oatmeal with toast or cold cereal with fruit, but
on weekends and night breakfasts, Gummy laid out a buffet.

After supper, Arnetta cleaned up the kitchen, her usual
task since she turned ten-years-old. Over the years, the job
got a little more involved. It started with helping to clear
the table, then rinsing dishes, then drying and putting away

the dishes. Gummy and Papaw didn't have a dishwasher because Papaw said he had a perfectly good dishwasher already, and she never broke down.

Thank goodness her homework wasn't too hard, because she couldn't get her mind off L.M., the mirror, and most of all, what she had seen in the mirror. It was so real except for the fact that it wasn't. If it had been real, she would've heard the crash, she would've seen the wrecked blue car, and the knocked over parking meter. She shivered, just thinking about it. She looked down at her science book. *I better get busy. Mrs. Griffin will have a test tomorrow. She calls them pop-quizzes, but the whole idea behind a pop-quiz is the element of surprise. Sort of hard to do when it happens like clockwork every Friday.* Arnetta was an average student with good grades. The good grades didn't come easy, but she enjoyed the challenge of studying on her own. Biology and Literature were her favorite subjects. It didn't hurt that Craig Walker was in both of those classes. He had been in her classes for a few years, but not until this year did it ever occur to her that he was the slightest bit interested in her. They shared a lab table in Biology class. Amazing what you can share about yourself while dissecting a frog. He thought the dissections would gross her out like some of the other girls, but it turned out she liked it better than he did.

CHAPTER FIVE

Craig had teased her, holding his hands up in mock surrender, "Remind me never to get on your bad side, Arnetta, or too close to you with that scalpel in your hand." The thought of him being close to her in any way, shape, or form made her blush. She was seldom speechless, but when she was next to Craig, words had a way of escaping her brain, except when it had to do with the subject at hand. Biology.

Her mind kept wandering, but it wasn't her fault. *Between Craig, tomorrow's test, and that dad-blamed mirror, how's a girl supposed to pay attention?* She thought about the accident. Not the accident in front of the What's New shop with the old blue car and the parking meter. The other accident. The accident no one in her household would dare bring up. Ever. The accident that changed everything. *I should've been with them.* Sometimes, she wished she *had* been with them. She remembered it like it was yesterday. What started as a typical family fun day went terribly wrong in an instant.

6

The Accident

May 13, 1977. Friday the thirteenth. Not that she's ever been superstitious, but Friday the thirteenths always made her more cautious since that day. It was like a movie that showed unwanted re-runs through her mind and couldn't be erased. She had been cast a starring role but would give anything if there could be a remake with a different ending.

May thirteenth happened to fall exactly one week between her and her brother's birthday. James came first; he had just turned ten-years-old that year. James had also been named for Etta James and James Arness. He got the easy one, out of those names, he just got the James. His full name was James Nathaniel Price. He got the name Nathaniel from his Papaw, Arnetta's daddy's father. Papaw and Gummy lived about three hours away in Landreth, SC, so they didn't see them very much, mostly just at Christmas, and that was always a rushed one-day visit.

Arnetta, James, and their parents lived in the same house as her other grandparents. The nice ones. Her mother's parents. Granma and Granpa Jones had just bought a house in Florida near the ocean. They said they were super excited about their upcoming move, except for the leaving us behind part. Granma and Granpa gave their house to Mama and Daddy. When they were gone, the plan was to turn their old bedroom into a den with another television, a sofa and maybe even a pool table if there was room after Arnetta and James brought in their favorite toys and bookshelves filled with their well-loved books. They'd also planned summer vacations spent at Granma and Granpa Jones' house. Arnetta remembered crying when she heard the news. Granma reached her arm around her so tight Arnetta couldn't help but feel she and Granma were one person. Granma Jones asked, "Arnetta, imagine a whole summer at the beach at our new house. It's right on the beach! You can do anything you want. We will have so much fun!" She'd enlarged her grasp to pull James into a group hug, "And James, you wouldn't believe the shells on the beach, and fishing off the pier? Somebody has to keep Granpa in line with his fish stories!" Arnetta thought it was a grand idea but couldn't help but notice a big fat tear trying to escape Granma Jones' eyes.

They had been planning a trip to Riverbanks Zoo in Columbia for weeks. All six of them would be going. They had plenty of room in the minivan and would have loads of fun. Her parents had gotten off work the whole day, and they planned to leave the house just after daybreak. It only took about two hours to get there, but Daddy had also arranged a tour of the Capitol that morning. They only had a couple of days to choose from because her grandparents were scheduled to move the next weekend, and James had to have a weekend to get ready for his summer camp starting Memorial Day Weekend. Their May calendar was so full, it barely had room for the numbers. Plans are good, but Arnetta changed those plans. She remembered that day, vividly.

After she woke up that morning, she looked over at the backpack she had packed for the trip. It had everything she wanted to take, but she took everything out just to be sure. She had her Cabbage Patch Doll she had gotten as an early eighth birthday present, a couple of books, and her favorite car pillow, the blue satin one. She was so excited! It was her first trip to the Zoo in Columbia. She hadn't slept well the night before and had gotten up earlier than usual on what the calendar indicated in red letters, Zoo Day, but to Arnetta, it felt like Christmas. She got up and started to put on the clothes her mother had laid out for her the night before. She was all dressed except for her socks and tennis shoes. That was the first time in her life she had remembered having a funny feeling inside. Like butterflies, only they were swarming, more like caged birds trying to escape. She went down the hall to tell her mama, but before she could get there, she exploded. No warning, well except for the butterflies. Nasty foul-smelling and even worse tasting vomit was all over the floor and on her clothes. It had surprised her so much, she just started screaming. Her mama, daddy, and James all came running, and they all reached Arnetta about the same time, except James, who stopped short when he saw the floor.

"Gross, Netta!" James always called her Netta. She always liked that; except that day, it didn't sound very nice.

"What's wrong, Honey?" my Daddy was kneeling and hugging me, vomit and all, while my Mama made a quick detour to the bathroom to get a wet washcloth to wipe my face.

"I don't know. I'm sorry!" Arnetta started to cry with big heaving wails that caused her body to shake.

"Don't be sorry, sweetie." Her mama had soothed, "You're just excited, that's all. Now, let's go get you cleaned up."

Just as they all started towards the bathroom, the other end exploded. Again, no warning. That time James ran down the hall and out the back door. Arnetta wished she could go with him. Her parents stayed right there with her and helped her get all cleaned up. They tucked her in bed and put a plastic pail by her bed and a cold, damp washcloth hanging over the side in case she felt sick again. They tried to tell her, as calmly as you can to an eight-year-old how to pay attention to the warning signs so she would have enough time to reach the bathroom. "But honey, if you can't make it, it's all right," they'd said.

She could hear her parents' muffled conversation from the next room while they cleaned up the hallway with Lysol and pine cleaner. The house smelled like a hospital. They were talking about waiting until the next day to go to the Zoo and skip the Capitol tour, and what if they waited to see how she was feeling in an hour or so, or what if they should just call the whole thing off, etc. Again, Arnetta helped make their decision for them when she got sick three more times that morning. Her doctor had called in a prescription and told them to keep her calm and in bed for a day or two with plenty of liquids, no solid food for a few days. It was probably just a stomach bug and may not be contagious, but to be on the safe side, she shouldn't be around other children.

She heard her parents talking to someone on the phone, she slept some, and then they all came into her room. All of them. Her mama, daddy, James, and Granma and Granpa Jones. Then came the preacher and his wife. She didn't know what was going on, but something was up, she could feel it in her bones.

Mama spoke first, "Now, Arnetta honey, first of all, we all want you to know you are going to be OK in just a little while. The doctor said so."

Then Daddy knelt beside her bed, "Arnetta, we don't want you to be mad at us, but we've decided to stick with the plan. We're going on to Riverbanks. We can take you to the zoo when you get better." He turned and looked at James and added, "Without James." He winked at the preacher and his wife standing on the other side of the bed, "Now, Preacher Campbell and Mrs. Lois are going to stay here and look after you until we get back. He's promised not to make you listen to any preaching."

Arnetta felt so bad. All she could do was look up at them. She wanted to go more than anything, but she could hardly hold up her head. She managed a little smile and said, "OK," then closed her eyes. Her Daddy took her hand, and her Mama put her hand on Arnetta's forehead and brushed her hair back, just like she did every night when she tucked her into bed. They both told her they loved her, and Arnetta answered in a faint whisper, "I love you, too." And then Arnetta fell in a deep dark hole of sleep.

Sleeping soundly until late afternoon when she rolled over and heard a soft crunch. She opened her eyes and saw a sheet of folded paper. Through blinking eyes, she unfolded it to see that James had colored a picture of a big smiley face with the words Have a happy day Netta. At eight years old, smiley faces always made her smile. She felt a little better as she sat up and padded her way down the hall. It felt like morning, but sun flooding through the French doors in the dining room told her it wouldn't be too long before sunset. Mrs. Campbell met her at the kitchen entrance and gave her a little hug.

"Arnetta! I'm so glad you're up and about. Did you sleep well? Here, honey, have a seat. I've been waiting for you to wake up. I've got something good for you to eat. Do you feel like eating anything?" Mrs. Campbell was like that. She talked and talked. The preacher's wife asked questions but kept on talking without giving anybody a chance to answer them. By the time she finished speaking, seemingly waiting on an answer, one wouldn't know which question to answer, even if they had remembered there was a question buried in her monologue. She continued, "Here, honey, here's some applesauce and chicken noodle soup. I removed all the noodles because the doctor said no real solids today. I don't think applesauce constitutes a solid, I sure hope not, don't you? Just take little sips and bites, dear. You must let your stomach know you're the boss, but you have to sneak up on it, or it may try to bite you back like it did this morning. Your mama and daddy will be so glad to know you're up and feeling a little bit better. They're supposed to call me in between the Capitol and the zoo." Mrs. Campbell's eyes darted toward the tangerine mosaic wall clock. "I know they're missing you, but I hope they're having fun and forgot, or probably can't find a reliable phone booth. Half the time, those things don't work, or they've been vandalized. What in the world is this world coming to? Now that you're up, when the phone rings, you can answer. Won't that be a surprise? They'll be so happy you're feeling better."

Arnetta sipped her soup from the side of the spoon, the way her Granma Jones taught her. She daydreamed about sipping soup with her Granma on an outside table overlooking the ocean. The daydream stopped there because there was a knock at the front door. The dining room had a wall of windows with sheer curtains allowing light to enter and a muted view of the street, just beyond their yard. Arnetta ate a bite of applesauce, while Mrs. Campbell made her way to the door. In her recollected memory, Arnetta heard the second hands on the wall clock ticking slower than usual. One-Mississippi TICK, two-Mississippi TICK, three-M-i-s-s-i-s-s-i-p-p-i TICK. Arnetta saw the black-and-white car out front, just as Mrs. Campbell saw the uniformed officer at the front door before she ever opened it.

Arnetta stayed in the dining room, but when she heard Mrs. Campbell shriek, she ran into the living room to see what the commotion was. Mrs. Campbell stood there with both hands covering her mouth, making little whimpering sounds. The policeman came in and was trying to console her, asking her who he could call to come to stay with them. Then they both looked at Arnetta. In her mind's playback, it was another forever captured, slow-motion moment.

They were looking at her like they were terrified of her but wanting to help at the same time. Arnetta felt like a lamb caught in a bear trap. In that instant, even an eight-year-old girl knew. She knew something had gone terribly wrong. The policeman thought Mrs. Campbell was a family member, and he told her there had been a tragic accident on Highway 78.

No one had made it out alive. There were no survivors.

No one had made it out alive. There were no survivors.

No one had made it out alive. There were no survivors.

Arnetta hadn't heard anything after that. Her ears were ringing. All she could hear was a high-pitched tone, and that phrase *no one had made it out alive.* There were no survivors. It had been seven years later before Arnetta found out the details of the accident. She had always wanted to know, but Gummy and Papaw said it didn't matter. It happened, and nothing good would ever come from her knowing exactly how they died that day.

When Arnetta was fifteen, Gummy had been sick, and Arnetta stayed home from school to care for her along with Papaw. It seemed to comfort Gummy to know she was there, so Arnetta stayed with her in her bedroom. Gummy slept and then slept some more. Arnetta got restless and decided to put away some of Gummy's laundry. She went into her Gummy's closet for the first time she'd ever remembered, as her grandparent's room had always been off-limits. When she slid over some hanging clothes on the metal rod to make room for more, she saw a box on a back shelf. The white-cardboard storage container was marked in magic marker ARNETTA. Hmmmph. *What's this?* She peeked out of the closet, and after assuring herself Gummy was still resting, she slid the shoe box off the shelf and through the opening she'd made in the fresh ironed shirts. *What's the big deal? It has my name on it. Don't tell me Gummy has been keeping my school papers and pictures for me.* Lifting the box top off, she saw something that nearly took all her breath. The one rescued breath resulted in a collective gasp, and she moaned as she lowered herself into a crisscross position in Gummy's closet. It was as if her life went from slow motion to a fast speed, but she was going in reverse. Faster and faster, she was being sucked into the past. The box held answers. Answers she had been wanting to know for a long time. *Inside this box is who I was. Inside this box was my world that was destroyed as if hit by a meteor. How much time did they have before they were obliterated? What were their last thoughts? Did they think of me? Inside this box is who I am.* Arnetta sat and read the newspaper clippings and the police report from May 13, 1977.

Her Mama had been driving. She was passing a logging truck when a log came loose and fell off the trailer. The statement from the logging truck driver said, "*It all hap-*

pened so fast. It was just a terrible freak accident." Another report stated: *When the log fell onto the highway, it had actually missed the van by inches, but the truck driver over-corrected when he realized what was happening, and jack-knifed his rig sandwiching the van between the cab and trailer. All the logs started to come off and littered the road, and one of them came through the van's windshield. The front seat passenger was decapitated. The driver and a female in the middle seat were also killed upon impact. An adult male and adolescent male were treated for injuries but died at the scene.*

Arnetta delved deeper in the box and found an envelope with a gold cross necklace, and five rings inside. She held the necklace up by the chain while the cross swung. A memory flashed across her mind of her mama leaning across her bed, saying what would be that last goodbye. The cross was dangling between them. She picked up the rings and tried to remember but couldn't. There were two thin and two large gold bands and a dainty diamond gold ring. The tears started to flow as she clutched the rings and necklace. She didn't know which rings belonged to her grandparents, and which ones belonged to her parents, but she held them as tight as she could trying to feel a connection to them. All she felt was cold metal. This box contained her past and her future.

Maybe Papaw and Gummy were right. Maybe I didn't need to know all that, what good is it to know? Maybe Gummy put all this back so that someday when she thinks I'm ready, she'll give them to me. And what day would that be, Gummy? What day could anyone ever be prepared for something like this? I wasn't ready then, and I'm not ready now. She put the things back like she found them in the box, stood, and returned the box to its hiding place with an angry shove. *Well, ain't that easy? Just go back on the shelf where you belong. You shouldn't have left me. You left me!* Before the tears came again, she returned the over starched shirts to their place and stepped out of the closet, quietly closing the door so she wouldn't wake her still-sleeping Gummy. She passed Papaw as she walked out the front door and said in his direction, "I'm going for a walk. Gummy's resting. I need some fresh air."

7

New Life

The morning after the accident, Preacher and Mrs. Campbell packed up a few things and delivered Arnetta to Gummy and Papaw's house in Landreth. Arnetta's relationship with her grandparents had gotten a little better over the years, but even now, eight years later, it was a distant relationship at best. She thought about her family every day. Arnetta had a fear that her memories would fade like the old Polaroid pictures in her keepsake box. The box was a little Lane cedar keepsake box, meant for her eighth birthday. She hadn't gotten it until Christmas that year though. Mrs. Campbell found the wrapped box when she'd returned from dropping Arnetta off and had packed it up with the rest of Arnetta's things. Gummy had thought it best to save it for Christmas, but she'd had no idea there was a note inside. The note was from her Mama and remained inside the box still. Arnetta took it out and read it from time-to-time.

Arnetta, I hope you like this keepsake box. Your Daddy and I picked it out just for you for your birthday. You can keep special things in here, like a special piece of jewelry, or little mementos from special occasions. This is your first box, and we hope you will keep it forever. In just a few years, on your sixteenth birthday, we will give you a much larger version and it will become your hope chest, just like the one in my room. We love you so much Arnetta, you are a shining light to everyone you meet, and we thank God every day that you are a part of this family. XOXOXOXO Mama and Daddy.

Gummy and Papaw never saw the note because Arnetta never shared it with them. The note, the box, her Cabbage Patch doll, and the last-minute smiley face picture from James were sacred to her and were safely tucked away in the little box. Everything except the Cabbage Patch doll, which was captured in four Polaroid pictures taken the day she received her doll the day before the Riverbanks Zoo trip. The well-loved doll now sat on top of her chest of drawers. Maybe if she held onto these things, she would never forget her family. She could think of nothing worse.

That very first Sunday, Gummy and Papaw took her to their church, the Candy Street Baptist church. They sat near the back. They stood for the hymns, but neither of them sang. They only went to big church, and she realized the next Sunday and the next that Gummy and Papaw didn't go every Sunday, and they only went to the morning preaching service. Her real family went every Sunday to a big Baptist church in Greenwood, SC. They went for Sunday School, preaching, then went back at night for Training Union and another service, and usually went to the Wednesday night prayer meetings after the mission meetings where they separated off by age groups. Arnetta had just started Girls in Action or GAs, and James was in Royal Ambassadors, or RAs. They had to stay late on Wednesday nights because both her parents were in the choir, and choir practice was after prayer meeting.

Most of the songs were the same in both churches, and Arnetta had remembered at least the chorus and would sing loudly despite the silent statues standing on either side. One of her favorite songs was Count your Blessings. The chorus was something like, 'Count your blessings, name them one by one, count your many blessings see what God has done'. *I know I have had many, many blessings in my life, most of them the first eight years of my life. Gummy and Papaw are blessings too, I have all the necessities I need, a roof over my head, clean clothes to wear, and food to eat. Oh my gosh, I'm starting to sound like Gummy!*

Arnetta had never pushed the limits like some of her friends when it came to clothes. Gummy would take her clothes shopping two or three times a year at a mall in Greenville, SC. Arnetta never demanded all the new rage in brand clothing. At school, kids were showing up in the latest fashion label, Tommy Hilfiger jeans. Gummy put her foot down on designer jeans. *There's no way I'm going to pay more than nineteen-ninety-five for a pair of dungarees. Why, when I was growing up, the only people that wore dungarees, or blue jeans as you call them, were field laborers, farmers and factory workers. Why you children want to walk around looking like the hired help is beyond me.* Arnetta had all the necessities, better than some, but certainly not as good as the cool people. Gummy had told her on many occasions, *"there will always be people that have more than you, Arnetta. But remember, there will always be people that don't have as much as you either. Those are the ones you should set your sights on, the less fortunate. Always try to find someone that has less than you and bring them up to your standards. Just think if everybody did that? Wouldn't this world be a better place to live in?"* Well, she had a point there.

Gummy was old, but Papaw was ancient. When Arnetta's daddy was born, Gummy was already forty years old and Papaw was forty-four. Now, they were seventy-four and seventy-eight. Luckily, Arnetta's parents had started a little earlier. James was born in 1967, and Arnetta followed in 1969. Their parents had married in 1966, and both were the same age, twenty-six.

It's like Gummy and Papaw were a walking encyclopedia of the way it used to be. Arnetta never could understand why they didn't try to figure out how to make it work the way it is now, but she figured it was a losing battle. She bet other girls her age didn't have to go through with lectures like she did. She never talked about her Gummy and Papaw to kids at school, she figured she'd be a laughingstock if she did.

When she was in elementary school, each class would have parties a few times a year. Arnetta never volunteered Gummy. It's not that she was ashamed of her, it's just that, well, maybe she was just a little embarrassed. She remembered the one time she volunteered Gummy for one of the grade mothers. In walked the bouncy Mrs. Lott, the blonde beauty queen who was Misty's mother, with her famous brownies, then Mrs. Kincaid, the dance instructor with the pony-tailed, red hair, who was Loreli's mother whom always brought potato chips and dip, and then here comes Gummy, scarf covered, gray-haired Gummy bringing her stinky egg salad sandwiches, and she wouldn't have even cut the edges off! Arnetta brought herself to the present for a moment. *Well, of course not silly. Cutting the edges off bread is wasteful. Waste not want not. I've heard that a million times.*

Pushing the limits under Gummy's rule was something she avoided like the plague, or else she'd be subject to one of her lectures. Arnetta had named them over the years, the words may be a little different from time to time, but the gist was always the same. The lectures lasted anywhere from the retelling of one of Gummy's old-wives-tales, or if she was lucky, just a one liner quote, like *Cleanliness is next to Godliness* or *A penny saved is a penny earned,* but sometimes it took what seemed like an hour to hear her out. If she got fidgety, or interrupted, or God forbid, Arnetta tried to do something else while listening, even homework, she may be subjected to a twofer, two lectures in the same session. Arnetta logged the top ten lecture topics in her brain, proof that repetition works. When Arnetta learned about Pavlov's dog in Science class, she recognized all too well the theory of conditioning. She'd never forget the top ten, not even if she tried. Of course, Gummy never knew her words had been memorialized as numbered passages like scriptures in a well-worn Bible. She wasn't entirely sure Gummy even realized how many times she repeated herself, but one of Arnetta's coping skills was to recall the lecture number while not rolling her eyes and showing mocked interest while zoning out for the duration. She'd taught herself to listen subconsciously for the tone of Gummy's voice to know when it was over. I *wonder how many hours, weeks, or even months I've wasted hearing her hogwash over the years?* Some quotes may have been her own, she used to think they all were, but over the years Arnetta learned some were quotes by Mark Twain, Benjamin Franklin, Johann Wolfgang Goethe, Thomas Jefferson and others. Whatever the intent of the quote, Gummy had made them her own by adding stories. There were more than ten, but the most used were forever ingrained in her mind as:

#1 KINDNESS- You can't be kind too soon, because you never know when too soon will be too late.

#2 HONESTY- Honesty is the first chapter in the book of wisdom. Or, if you always tell the truth, you won't have to remember as much. Or, Honesty IS the best policy.

#3 CLEANLINESS- Cleanliness is next to Godliness.

#4 FRIENDSHIP- A friend in need is a friend indeed.

#5 PUNCTUALITY- punctuality is the duty of regular people, and the politeness of kings.

#6 RESPONSIBILITY- Never put off until tomorrow what can be done today.

#7 THRIFTINESS- A penny saved is a penny earned. Or, waste not, want not.

#8 KNOWLEDGE- Experience is the best knowledge.

#9 FAIRNESS- It is not fair to ask of others what you are unwilling to do yourself.

#10 HONOR- It is not doing the thing we like to do but liking the thing we have to do that makes life blessed.

No, Gummy and Papaw didn't attend church regularly, but they had their heads screwed on right, I guess. I am blessed to have them in my life, I just wished a family feeling would be there sometimes. There were never any nighttime tuck-ins, bye-love-yous, or hand holding. *Not that I need or want them now, but a tuck-in-the-bed wouldn't have hurt them, would it?* Being tucked into bed each night was one of the things she missed the most after coming to live with Gummy and Papaw. Her mama and daddy either took turns, or both came in every night to tell her how much they loved her, made sure she had brushed her teeth, read a short story from a book she got to pick out, said nighttime prayers with her and finished with a soft kiss in the same spot on her forehead, uncovered when they brushed her bangs back with their hand. Every night. Every night without fail. The first night at Gummy's house and all the nights that followed, Arnetta had gone to bed alone. Many nights she had cried herself to sleep. Some nights still.

8

See I Told You

Monday after school, Arnetta caught a ride with Amy Perkins. She had to go to the dentist's office or else get another lecture on responsibility. Landreth High was only about a mile from town, but when she'd mentioned dreading having to go back to the dentist just to get her raincoat, Amy had offered. Since the storm last Thursday, the weather seemed to have decided it was winter after all, and Amy was glad she'd worn her purple puffer jacket on top of her turtleneck. On the quiet ride, she was trying to figure out how she would manage to wear the raincoat on top of her other clothes without looking like the Michelin man. Her hooded slicker was flannel lined and a little bulky, *there's no way I can wear both at the same time. I guess I can wear one over my arm, neither will fit in my backpa...*

"Earth to Arnetta. Arnetta?"

"Huh?

Amy was pulling over to the side of the road near the intersection of Collier and Memorial Drive, almost right in front of Dr. Wilmer's office. "Is this OK?

"Yeah, yeah, this is great. Thanks, Amy. Sorry, I sort of spaced out a little. In deep thought, I guess."

"Such deep thoughts for such a shallow mind, tsk, tsk." Amy had both hands on the steering wheel but was turned towards Arnetta with an exaggerated mocked concern look on her face.

Arnetta opened the car door. "Ha, Ha. Yep, you could throw a penny in, but it'd bounce back." Amy was a good school friend. Since Arnetta didn't drive yet, it was good to have a friend with wheels. Amy looked for any excuse to get out and drive, and since most people gave her a buck or two for gas money, she had spending money.

Arnetta was leaning in the car door to tell Amy thanks, but Amy spoke first, "So.... what were you in such deep thought about? Craig? I hear he's got..."

Both girls looked down the street after hearing a loud BAM! It sounded like something fell from the sky onto the road.

Arnetta heard Amy finish her sentence with an unintended "What in the world?" When Amy would turn to Arnetta, she wouldn't get an answer because she was gone. Arnetta was running down the street right towards the noise. It was a crash, it had to be. She wasn't the only one going to check it out, people seemed to be coming out of the woodwork like ants at a picnic. It reminded Arnetta of the boys at school talking about the Sunday NASCAR races when the fans rubbernecked to see any sign of a wreck.

She was starting to give out of breath when she reached the scene and saw a blue Gremlin had jumped the curb and knocked over the parking meter. Arnetta stopped short and felt that feeling in the pit of her stomach. A lady was walking down the street who had almost been hit. She probably would've been if she hadn't been paying attention. Arnetta was one of the first to get there, and the policeman was helping someone out of the car. All Arnetta saw at first was blood. Blood and black hair. She turned to see the shaken pedestrian standing next to that little man, L.M. Arnetta's eyes widened as they looked at each other with a knowing stare. Arnetta's eyes panned the situation with a surreal slow motioned turn of her head. L.M. The green awning of the What's New Shop. The parking meter. The blue car. The policeman had gotten someone out of the vehicle, and that someone was a girl with long black hair. The girl locked eyes with Arnetta about the same time Arnetta's knees started to give way. She had to sit down. She reached behind her so her hands could help guide her to the curb.

"Miss, Miss, are you all right? Did you get hurt? Were you in the car?"

Arnetta looked up, but the sun was in her eyes. All she could see was a big black blob. She blinked, but the sun was right behind the blob, so she only got a silhouette. The blob was talking. Talking a lot.

"No. I'm fine. I wasn't.... what happened?"

Arnetta saw the light when the blob moved away, allowing the full sun to bear down on her. Dangit! The blob was walking toward the policeman.

"Miss, what's your name? Did you see what happened? Did you get hit? Are you OK? The policeman took the blob's place with the sun behind him. She couldn't see his face, only the shape of his hat. The way he was turning his head after each question made the sunlight appear like a strobe light. Looking to see why he was moving his head like a metronome, she understood. He kept turning to look at the girl with black hair. She was with the other policeman. Arnetta managed to catch a glimpse between two people standing way too close to her. She couldn't stop looking at the girl, and the girl was staring right back at her. *I'm going to be sick if I don't get up.*

She heard a familiar voice. It was L.M. "Excuse me, hey, let me through, pardon me..."

Arnetta realized she had created a scene, and people were now standing around her. HER of all people. Not the girl that had been driving the car, or the lady who was almost hit, but her. L.M. made it through and was now standing in front of her. Even though she'd barely met him, he seemed like an old friend.

"Arnetta, you OK? Come on, let's stand you up. C'mon inside the store and sit down a bit, OK?" He held out his hand, and she graciously accepted it.

"OK. I d-didn't mean to cause a commotion. I just wanted to...Hey, did you see what happened, L.M? Did you get a load of that parking meter?" L.M. didn't say a word until they walked into the What's New shop. After being in the sun, it was like stepping from day into the night.

"Yes. I saw." He said while directing her to the same chair she sat in four days ago. "It's happened before, well not in front of my place, mind you, but it's happened. Why just a few years ago, a little girl was hurt very badly when an old man got his brakes and gas pedal mixed up, jumped the curb, but instead of a parking meter, he knocked over a person. That little girl almost lost a leg! She had many surgeries, and I'm sure a lot of pain and was left disfigured, but it didn't stop her. She grew up to become a nurse. That old man shouldn't have been driving. I always wondered if she went into nursing because of the trauma she'd suffered." L.M. seemed to come back to the present situation as he gave a slight shake of his head and then craned his neck to study the scene through his storefront window. "I don't know what that girl's problem was. Why she looks like she isn't more than your age if she's a day."

Arnetta joined him at the window. Only a few onlookers remained. An ambulance had arrived, and one attendant was taking care of the girl, while another was assessing the lucky lady who had barely missed getting hit. L.M. turned to Arnetta, "Wait here, I'll see if I can find out what's going on."

Arnetta watched him sort of work the crowd. He didn't talk to anyone, just casually listened while walking around observing other people. He came back inside and gave Arnetta a small smile. "Turns out the lady is fine, just a little shaken. The black-haired girl wasn't hurt that bad either, just a whole lot more shook up. Her forehead has a nasty goose egg, a gash below her eye, and she broke her nose. That's where all the blood came from. I heard the attendant told her that head wounds always have a lot of blood." They both watched as the attendants strapped her on a gurney and wheeled her towards the ambulance.

"I thought you said she wasn't that bad- why are they putting her in an ambulance?"

L.M. patted her shoulder, "I also heard them tell her they were taking her to the hospital for observation. She'll be OK, Arnetta. She'll be OK."

Landreth only had one hospital, and it was only a few blocks away. That's one of the good things about living in a small town; everything was practically within walking distance. Landreth was sort of set up like a six-pointed star. Main Street was the center, then three streets shot off to smaller roads that led to areas with the textile mill, the mill village, car repair places, a few small churches, doctor offices, pharmacies, and the hospital. On the other side of Main Street were the other three areas with Landreth Country Club, a couple of car dealerships, three big old churches, the library, and Landreth Mall with a J.C. Penney at one end, and a Sears at the other. The schools, all three of them, were on this side of the star too. Arnetta always wished one day she'd see Landreth from up above. Each point of the star all met on Main Street. Of course, there were lots of roads here and there, but the main roads all led you back to town. Landreth was like a little galaxy in the grand scheme of things.

"L.M. I want to go see her. Now. I want to go see her at the hospital."

"Arnetta, you don't even know her. It will take them a little time to get her situated. They may not even have to keep her. Sometimes they just need to make sure she doesn't have a concussion or anything like that. If she does, they may keep her for a few hours or overnight to make sure she doesn't go to sleep."

"I'm going" Arnetta was glaring at L.M. She couldn't believe he could be so calm. "You don't have to if you don't want to, but it was your store that she almost ran into. Don't you want to know why?"

They both turned to look out the window again when they heard a loud motor running. There was a tow truck hooking up the blue Gremlin by the back to get it into the road. There was a logo on the side of the rusty red truck. It was faded, but she'd memorized it over the years. The circular logo was a little man with a big head holding one of his hands up, the top of the arc quoted, "When your car lets you down, and the lower arc read, "Akers is the best in town." Arnetta always wondered if that logo really helped business, or if they got business because they were the only tow-service in town.

L.M. looked at Arnetta, "Why do you want to go to the hospital? You're not hurt. You don't know that girl that *was* hurt either. Why are you so hellfire, bent, and determined to go to the hospital?"

"Admit it, L.M. You want to go too. Don't you? You want to go check on her as much as I do. Go ahead, admit it."

"I do no such thing. Sometimes it's best not to go meddling in other people's affairs."

Arnetta heard the grinding of the tow chain being let down from the tow truck. The man from Akers Tow Service had gotten the wrecked car off the curb and was able to back it out onto the street. Now, he was getting ready to attach the front of the car's bumper to the large metal hook so he could haul it behind his truck to the repair shop. The grinding and clinking chain reminded Arnetta of what an old ship may have sounded like while letting out its anchor. Too bad that girl's car couldn't have let out an anchor before she lost control and jumped the curb. Otherwise, she would have had smooth sailing. Out of the corner of her eye, she saw a familiar face.

"Oops." She muttered.

"What now?" L.M. asked.

"It's my friend, Amy. I think she's looking for me." With that, Arnetta jumped up, and out of the chair, she'd been resting in, and walked over to the front door, opened it, but held onto the door handle as she popped her head out.

"Amy. Amy, over here."

"Arnetta? What are you doing? I've been waiting for you. I didn't know where you ran off to. I saw the ambulance; did you see what happened?"

Arnetta stepped out, and closed the door behind her, but stayed on the broad brass threshold underneath the awning. "No, I don't know, not really. Some girl jumped the curb in that piece of junk," as she pointed to the Gremlin. "Look at the parking meter, that's the only fatality. She must've been speeding to knock that thing off its base like that." The meter was lying on the sidewalk. The pole was bent a little, but the bottom had cracked the base around the concrete, and there was a big chunk of cement still attached. It reminded Arnetta of an escaped prisoner caught while trying to make a run for it. Conquered with a ball and chain around its feet.

Amy looked at the fallen meter, to Arnetta, and then towards her car. "Well, if you're going to Dr. Wilmer's office, you'd better hurry. Your raincoat, remember?"

"Oh, yeah, that had completely slipped through my brain, Amy. Thanks."

Arnetta stepped out to the edge of the curb and looked down the street. "But you know what? I'll just walk from here, and I'll walk home too. Thanks for the ride, Amy. You'd practically had me at the front door a while ago." Arnetta instinctively reached for her backpack to get her wallet. "Oh wait, I'll need to walk back with you anyway. I forgot my backpack in your car." She looked back in the store window, but she couldn't see anything past her reflection. She turned back to Amy and held up her index finger, "Wait just one minute, please, I forgot something in there."

Arnetta found L.M. right where she left him. *Has he been spying on me?*

"L.M., I've got to go to the dentist's office."

"Again?"

"Well, yes. I forgot my raincoat there last Thursday, remember?" *It's the only reason I came into this store, to begin with, but I better not divulge that part. He may take it the wrong way. I don't want to hurt his feelings, and besides, I'm still hoping he'll take me to the hospital.* Arnetta looked out the window at her friend waiting... almost patiently. "I was thinking, what if I get Amy to drop me off back here after I get my raincoat, and then we can go to the hospital?"

"What's this we stuff? I never said I was going to the hospital. Besides, I'm not sure it's appropriate."

"Appropriate?"

"Yes, well, we hardly know each other, and you're going to get in a car with a perfect stranger? What would your parents think?"

"Parents? I don't have parents, remember?" Arnetta couldn't remember how much, or if she had told him anything about her parents. "I live with my grandparents. They don't care what I do as long as I'm home by 6:00. Any later than that, and they call the Sheriff and the police." She said that last part with a little smirk. *I can take care of myself, but I guess he's got the point. I don't really know him at all. The simple thing would be to tell Amy about her plans, but I hadn't planned on telling Amy anything about the old blue car, the girl that was taken to the hospital, and especially about L.M. I've got to come up with a different plan.*

"Please, L.M.? We don't have to stay long, no more than thirty minutes tops. Please?"

L.M. looked over at one of the grandfather clocks along the wall. They looked more like sentry guards. Their heavy metal pendulums were marking time like soldiers marching along, keeping beat with the passing of each second. He looked back at Arnetta.

"OK. I would've been ready to close here within the hour anyway. By the time you go to the dentist to fetch your coat, I should be ready when you return." L.M. looked out towards Amy and continued, "But no more than thirty minutes at the hospital. I'm taking you at your word. Think your friend would like to come?"

"Who, Amy? No. No, I'm sure she wouldn't." Arnetta looked down for a couple of seconds, then faced L.M. while reaching for the big brass doorknob behind her, "She has piano lessons on Monday afternoons. She's in a bit of a hurry, or I would've asked her to begin with." *OK, well, that was a bald-faced lie, and something tells me L.M. knows it is, but what choice do I have? I don't want anyone at school to think I'm crazy.*

L.M. offered, "We don't have to go today, you know. You can catch up with that girl at school, can't you? You should give her time to rest up. She's been through quite a traumatic day. Did you see her face? You know that's got to hurt."

Knowing he was right about the girl's injuries and state of mind, but still, she just couldn't let it go. "L.M. Please? I need to see her today while everything is fresh in her mind. We won't stay. I've got to go. Amy's waiting on me I'll be back before you know it, OK?

"Well, I still don't know why you're so bent on going to see that girl, Arnetta. But I'll take you. I'll wait for you. Go.

Go on to the dentist. I'll be here when you get back. But you will tell your grandmother where you've been when you get home, won't you?

"Yeah, sure, I will. "

"Arnetta, I'm serious about this. No secrets. That's not a good way to start a friendship."

Friendship? Is that what he thinks this is? More like a partnership if you ask me. And no secrets? Who on earth does he think he's kidding? No secrets. Hmmmph. "OK. OK. I'll tell her. Promise." *I'm just not promising when I'll tell Gummy.* "You asked me why I want to go see that girl so bad..."

"Badly."

"Pardon?"

"You said, "You asked me why I wanted to go and see that girl so bad," it's badly. Don't they teach grammar at your school? And yes, I really would like to know before we go to the hospital, Arnetta."

"OK. Badly. Well, it's because this is all my fault."

"What? What's your fault? What do you mean?"

"The wreck, L.M. That's what I'm talking about. It's all my fault. I...I saw it."

"I saw it too, Arnetta. A lot of people saw it. There's nothing you could've done to prevent that accident."

"Yes, there is" Arnetta turned the knob she had been holding and opened the door. She held her free hand up in the air toward Amy and motioned with her index finger and mouthed one more minute. Amy put her hand on her hips, then raised her hands, palms up in a silent, why pose. Arnetta shook her one-more-minute gesture and shut the door.

L.M. gave Arnetta a one-sided grin, "Looks like you're about to lose that ride too. Glad I'm not the only one under your spell. You're one very persuasive young lady."

Arnetta marched over towards the vanity she had admired a few days before, searching for a particular item, the tan paddle mirror. *Did he sell it? I know it was right here. Wait. Is that it? What's this?* Arnetta picked up a handle and pulled off a green felt sleeve uncovering the intricate design she'd admired. "What's this?"

"Oh, I put the felt sleeve on there to protect it."

Looking at L.M. with clinched brows, she slipped the mirror back into its sleeve and gently returned it to its place. Then she picked up a smaller mirror and showed it to him, then she walked down the aisle, and every time she came to a hand mirror, she picked it up and showed it to L.M.

"Stop. What are you doing?"

"No Secrets, L.M.? Isn't that what you said?"

"Well, yes. That's precisely what I said."

"That accident was my fault because I saw it in that mirror." She pointed her head in the direction of the covered mirror. I saw it on Thursday, and it happened on Monday.

It happened just like I saw it. I'd say it's my fault. I should've been able to prevent it. I don't know how, but I should have. Please tell me what is so special about that particular mirror." It was more of a statement than a question.

"Arnetta, I don't think it's the mirror."

"What do you mean?"

"Just what I said. I don't think the mirror is any different than any mirror in here, but..."

"But what? Why is it the only one covered?"

"Please let me finish. I don't think the mirror is any different than any other mirror in here until you picked it up. I could be wrong. It may not be the mirror at all. It may just be you."

"What? Me? What do you mean? I've never seen anything like that before. I'm just an ordinary, regular girl." *Uh oh. There's that feeling again. Bees swarming. Check. Hairs prickling on the back of my neck. Check.* "I told you so."

"Now, what do you mean by I told you so?"

"I told you what I saw last week. You shrugged it off. I told you today the wreck was my fault, and it is because I saw it happen twice! I told you so." Arnetta turned and walked to the door, jerking the doorknob before the geyser inside of her exploded. *Control. Control. Get a grip Arnetta. There'll be no exploding today.* Once outside, she stopped short, stood there motionless for a second, inhaled and exhaled, and then consciously relaxed her shoulders.

CHAPTER EIGHT

With a smile, she turned to Amy, "Thanks for waiting, Amy."

As they walked towards Amy's car, Arnetta could feel Amy studying her, trying to get a read on her emotions. *I know we're not what you'd call best friends, but if I'm not careful, my reputation of being a normal girl is going to be shot straight to hell.*

9

Unspoken Words

Amy tried to start a conversation with Arnetta on the short drive to the dentist's office, in the parked car in front of Dr. Wilmer's office, and again when Arnetta returned to the car. She'd tried school subjects, the weather, and the funny sound Amy's car was starting to have just before it started. When none of those subjects worked, she tried the Craig Walker topic. There was no use, Arnetta was in her own world.

They were almost back to the What's New store. Arnetta planned to have Amy drop her off at the corner just beyond the store, and then she'd backtrack. *I'm not ready to try and explain who L.M. is or why I'm going back. As far as Amy knows, he's just a concerned citizen. He's just the person that helped her off the street when she felt lightheaded after seeing the accident. That's all she needs to know. I can't explain what I don't know myself, can I? Do I say L.M. is my new friend? An old friend? I've never really had a friend that was an old person before. It's not that I don't like old people, it's just sort of weird.* Arnetta heard Amy talking, but she was too deep in

thought to reply. She was thinking about her grandparents.
Gummy and Papaw don't really have close friends, so it's not
like I have a lot of experience around older people. They go out
to an occasional Christmas party, or to the mountains with a
busload from the church, but they keep to themselves most of
the time. Whole conversations are held with a Hmmph here,
and a similar grunt there, an extended arm offering a plate of
something with a raised eyebrow. It's sort of funny to watch.
When they get ready to go somewhere, they both just look at
each other until one of them, usually, Papaw makes eye con-
tact and heads for the door. According to the weather, Papaw
goes into the front closet and gets both of their jackets, hats,
or umbrella. He hands Gummy her coat while he puts on his,
then he helps her on with hers. All this time, not a word is spo-
ken. Not an 'it's about time to go,' or 'we should be going, here,
let me get your coat for you,' or 'it's supposed to start raining,
we should carry an umbrella.' Nope. Not a word. I'm not sure
if all married people get that way or not. I know when I was
little, I remember a beehive of activity swarming almost any-
time things were happening, not only one conversation, but
two at the same time. I wonder when Gummy and Papaw got
this way. Were they as silent when Daddy was growing up?
Or did they change when I came to live with them? I never
thought about it when I was younger, how much my coming
to live with them must have changed their lives. I knew how

my life was different, and I didn't like it. A different life. Not always rough, and not always smooth, just different.

Arnetta was aware that Amy was still talking. Up until now, it had been almost like background noise, but she caught the tail end of the monologue, and it struck a nerve.

Amy said, "Arnetta, you're scaring me. What's going on with you? Why aren't you talking to me? Who is that man you were talking to at the store?" A tiny bit of Amy's wrinkled brow was evident of her concern until she laughed and continued with, "He's weird, isn't he? And he's so little, what's wrong with him?"

Arnetta's head whipped towards her friend, "Amy shut up. Just shut up, OK?"

Amy straightened like she'd been struck with Arnetta's words.

"I'm sorry, Amy. I didn't mean that. I'm sorry. It's just that he's not a weird man, he's very nice actually. Have you ever been inside his store? The What's New Shop?"

"No, I haven't. Apology accepted. I guess. You didn't have to jump down my throat, though. And besides, why would I want to go to that store? It looks like another one of those stupid old stores with a bunch of junk in it. It's a junk store."

"No, it's not Amy. It's an antique and treasures shop." Arnetta felt herself flush, hearing her own words. *Why am*

I defending L.M. and his shop? I felt the same way just a few days ago.

Looking out the window, Arnetta noticed they were right in front of the What's New. Without turning her head back towards Amy, she said, "Stop the car."

"What? Here?"

"Yes. Here. Just let me out here. I'll walk home from here. There's something I want to do." Arnetta reached over into the back seat of Amy's Pinto and grabbed her raincoat and backpack. She dug into the larger of the two front pockets and pulled out a couple of loose dollars, folded them over and wedged them in between two of the cassette tapes that were stuck in between the front seats.

Amy stopped and pulled into a parking space. "Arnetta, you're sure? I don't mind waiting and taking you home after you *do what you gotta do.*" Amy used air quotes along with an attitude for the last part of her remark.

Arnetta didn't retaliate. *After all, I am a guest in Amy's car. She didn't have to give me a ride at all if she didn't want to, and I know I'll need another ride at some point. I better choose the sweet route. Put on your happy face, Arnetta, and pretend you didn't hear the hate in that last remark.* "No, that's OK, Amy, but thanks for the ride." Arnetta flashed another big smile as she got out of the car. Arnetta realized she and Amy weren't all that much different than Gummy and Papaw in a way. Maybe all relationships have their ways of communicating without always having to spell it out with spoken words.

She made a deal with herself right then and there to try to not only listen more to what people had to say but, more importantly, look and pay attention to what they weren't saying and what that meant.

10

The Wait

The hospital was almost two miles from Collier Street, so it was nice to have L.M. take her there. Even though it had been at least an hour since the accident, there was time to kill. The doctors hadn't decided on whether to admit the girl or release her. Arnetta and L.M. sat in the emergency room lobby and waited for the nurse to let them go back and visit. Arnetta had told a little white lie to have the chance to see the girl. *Maybe not an award for Best Actress, but I think I did OK.*

Arnetta approached the window where a nursing unit clerk sat. "I'd like to see the girl that just came in a little while ago."

"Are you family?" she'd asked without stopping her writing.

Well, no. I wasn't expecting that. "No, Ma'am. I'm not." *Think. Think. Think.* "But I'm all she's got right now."

The nursing unit clerk stopped writing, looked up and cocked her head, "Oh, is that so, huh, how's that?"

"She's in my class at school."

"And her name is....?"

"Well, that's just it. She's new, so I haven't learned her name yet, but I recognized her from school. I was there when it happened."

"When what happened?"

Arnetta stopped herself from rolling her eyes. "The wreck! I was there when the wreck happened. I need to check in on her." *Manners, Arnetta. Remember your manners.* "Please?"

"OK. But just a quick visit, and you'll have to wait a few minutes while they finish checking the patient."

"Thank you." Arnetta turned and walked back over to where L.M. was sitting. *Well, that wasn't so bad.*

While they were waiting, Arnetta picked up a copy of McCall's magazine and stared at the picture of Princess Diana on the cover. *She is so beautiful. A real fairy tale and a real Princess.* Arnetta scanned the front of the magazine for anything that she wanted to read. The Princess feature story was all about how to get her hairstyle, and secrets exposed by her hairdresser.

"A penny for your thoughts." L.M. almost whispered.

"Huh? Oh, nothing. Just catching up on current events."

"Hey, listen," L.M. leaned a little closer so the entire ER lobby world couldn't hear, "Earlier, you said something about living with your grandparents. I'm sorry, I didn't know."

"It's OK."

"Anything you want to talk about?"

"No, not really." Arnetta pulled the magazine closer, opened it, and pretended to read.

"That's too bad." He straightened up, turned to the table of magazines beside him, and picked up a six-month-old copy of U.S. News & World Report. "Look at this. I heard about this the other day. You'd think aliens were attacking the United States the way the media is all over this story about President Reagan." He loudly whispered the large print byline, "On July 13th, Vice President George H.W. Bush acted as President nearly twelve hours while President Reagan had a simple surgery."

"Interesting story?"

"Not really. I've read it before. As usual, the news media has to have something to write about. I'm just catching up on *my* current events, even if this is old news."

"Oh, just wondering."

"Wondering what?"

"Just wondering why you were asking about me living with my grandparents, that's all."

"I wanted to let you know if you needed to talk about anything, you could talk to me. You know, like an Uncle."

Arnetta sat up from her slumped position, "And why do you think I need to have someone to talk to? You know, like an Uncle?"

"Well, do you have anyone to go to that you can talk with? I mean besides your friends at school. Any teachers or anything?"

"Well, no. I guess not." Arnetta got quiet until she noticed a dreaded pause between them, "Hey, you're not some kind of weirdo, are you? Because if you are, you have to know I've told lots of my friends about you already, so if I turned up missing or anything..."

L.M. smiled. It started in the corners of his mouth, and then spread all over his face, his round cheeks pushing his eyes into little slits.

"What's so funny?"

"That sounds almost impossible."

"What does?"

"You. Turning up missing."

"Well. thanks a lot! What's that supposed to mean?"

"Well, if you *turned up*, his stubby fingers using air quotes for emphasis, "how could you still be missing?"

"You know what I mean. It's not funny either. I'm being serious."

"I'm sorry. Yes, I do know what you mean, and I shouldn't be making fun of your questions and concerns." L.M. straightened in his chair by using his arms. He pushed down on the armrests, lifting his body, shifting his weight towards Arnetta, his feet never reaching the floor. "I'm harmless, Arnetta. I just wondered because I was raised by an older couple in a group home."

"A what? What's a group home?"

"The best way to explain it, it's the next thing up from an orphanage. It was a boy's home. Most boys were sent there because they were too much trouble to handle at home, but there were plenty there who had no parents. Some of their parents were victims of war, disease, in jail, fell on bad times, or whatever."

"Which were you? Too much to handle or an orphan?"

"Neither actually. I guess I was sent there as an orphan by abandonment, but my mother showed up when I was seventeen years old. She had left me with a neighbor while she ran off with a traveling salesman."

"What? Really? How could she, I mean...and what about your father?"

"My father had already died. He was twenty years her senior, and I guess I just weighed her down too much, and she couldn't handle it. The grass is always greener, they say."

"Yeah, but still. How old were you?"

"I was only three years old. I was little, and my mother was still young and very impressionable. The older I got, I think my condition, as she called it, became more obvious, and she just couldn't take it. The traveling salesman didn't want her if she came with baggage, so she made her decision to drop off the baggage somewhere else so she could live her life. As a child, my only recollection of her was walking down the street with my hand in hers. I remember looking up at her, but she wouldn't look back."

"Oh my gosh, I think that's terrible! I'm so sorry!" *Geez, I had no idea. Poor L.M.*

"Oh, don't be. Forgive and forget. I did a long time ago." He made a fist and showed Arnetta his ring again. "I didn't know what I'd missed until she came back into my life, I was seventeen and had just finished high school. She had come into some money, enough money to send me to college. We kept in touch until she died about ten years later.

"Well, I still say that stinks, and I'm still sorry. Everybody has a story, don't they?"

"Yes, Arnetta. Yes, they do. Some aren't as dramatic as others, but everyone has a story."

Wow. At least my mother didn't dump me. And his father was so old, how would that have been for him? My parents both left me at the same time, but the timing wasn't their choice or mine.

11

The Girl In The Mirror

Arnetta and L.M. continued to talk while waiting. It was mostly small talk until L.M. brought up her parents.

"So, tell me, we've been talking about me an awful lot. Well, me and my mother. Why don't you tell me about *your* mother?"

As if on cue, the swinging door between the waiting room and the inner sanctum of the emergency room opened. A large pale-skinned nurse appeared. Her starched, white nurse's hat had a thin black stripe that went around the cuffed-up part. She sort of looked into the air, the way a blind person may look toward something, but never at anything. She wore a tight belted white dress, but the belt was up and over her rotund waist, more likely to hold up her boobs. When she spoke, it was more like a drone, like she was on autopilot.

"Family of Brinda Barefoot."

The nurse stood there and stared straight ahead as people in the lobby were starting to look from person to person.

"Brinda Barefoot family?" That time, there was a questioning tone in her voice.

Arnetta was looking around and saw no one rise to the call. Arnetta figured this was a going once, going twice, sorry no family here, you lose type request. *I better speak up and hope for the best.* Arnetta stood up but stayed in front of the uncomfortable, avocado green, vinyl chair she'd been squirming in for the last thirty minutes. The nurse was starting to turn around and close the door. *Oh, no, wait!*

"Excuse me? Nurse? Is Brinda Barefoot the girl that had a wreck on Collier Street a little while ago?"

"Well, that depends," the nurse cocked her head, and turned back toward the waiting room. "Are you the family of the girl that had a wreck on Collier Street a little while ago?"

"Yes, Ma'am," Arnetta looked at L.M. He was holding the U.S. News and World Report up in front of his lowered face. *Funny how interesting that magazine became suddenly.*

The nurse's lip turned up on one corner, letting Arnetta know that she was on to her little secret. *I bet these nurses are used to 'families' coming to check on the infirmed all the time.*

"Well, come on back then." Arnetta started for the door and then turned around to see if L.M. was coming. He wasn't.

"L.M.," she whispered hoarsely. He lowered the magazine, but held onto it, and gave her his raised eyebrow look as if saying, what? She had to smile because when he did that, his little wrinkled brow looked like a dog she'd seen in Time Magazine. A Shar- Pei, so ugly and wrinkly, it was cute. L.M's few strands of hair he insisted on combing over his almost bald head made the sight even funnier. She tried to compose herself before she laughed out loud. "Aren't you coming?"

"No, I'll wait out here. You go ahead."

Arnetta looked over towards the impatient nurse and walked with haste so as not to waste any more of her time. God forbid she misses her break or something. Giving the nurse the most polite smile she could muster, Arnetta whispered a thank you as she passed through the door.

The nurse introduced herself, "I'm Mattie. Brinda has a pretty nasty bump on her head. She's gonna need you to look at her sort of normal, OK? Don't go in there and get all *Oh My God* on me. She needs calm right now. Hear me?"

"Yes, Ma'am. Thanks for the warning. I saw all the blood earlier. It was a loud crash! I heard it all the way down the street. I ran down the block just after she knocked over the parking meter. Is she going to have to stay here the night?"

"I don't think so. We're just going to have to wait a bit and see. She's under observation. Now sometimes observations mean several hours, but we never know. I need you to fill out this form before you go in to see her."

"What is it?" Arnetta asked while taking the offered pen from Nurse Mattie.

"Oh, it's just a form listing visitors. Just put your name and address down there, something new we must do in the ER, no big deal. Supposed to help guarantee patient safety or something. It's always something. We've never had a problem yet, but I suppose that's the best way to avoid one, huh?"

Arnetta wrote in her name, address, and phone number on the form and handed the clipboard and pen back to the nurse as she continued their conversation.

"Oh, so she could be here overnight." They were making their way down a hallway made of curtained rooms. There were different smells as she walked by each one. Alcohol, the smell of disinfectant, a foul body odor, but the worst was yet to come. As they passed curtain number four, or maybe five, it was hard to tell because they all looked the same, the putrid smell of poop washed into Arnetta's nostrils like lava from a volcano. On instinct, she put her hand to her nose and squeezed. No use, it was bound to be there forever.

The nurse answered, "Well, yeah. I guess if you put it like that. I get off at 3 o'clock in the morning. I've been here since three this afternoon, so to me overnight, don't mean much. But, yeah, she could easily be here for a few more hours, or after I leave at shift change."

They finally reached the right curtain. Nurse Mattie reached her hand up and yanked the curtain back, making a scraping sound like a shower curtain as the rings slid across the metal rod. The girl was out cold and sort of half sitting up on the gurney, propped up with several pillows. *What a weird way to sleep. I wonder why she doesn't just fall on over, but she wouldn't get far with those rails pulled up. I almost didn't see them because they were covered with white sheets. White sheets, white pillows, and the girl is covered up to the waist with a white blanket. White, white, white, it really makes her stand out with her black hair and blue calico shirt. Man, I bet that shirt is toast. She'll never get all the bloodstains out. If it were mine, I could see Gummy cutting the buttons off to put in her button jar to keep for whenever someone needed a gazillion buttons. I bet any other time, the girl in bed eight would be considered beautiful in a natural kind of way. Her skin reminds me of the amber we studied in Science, and her hair spilled out over the pillow like a waterfall, except for the few sparkles caused by broken windshield glass caught up in the tangles of dried blood. Poor girl. I don't want to wake her up. Should I? I need to talk with her. I wish nurse Mattie would leave. Sort of. Feels kind of crazy just standing here with her over my shoulder.*

"Wow. That's a big light!" Arnetta pointed to the magnifier light attached to a looming metal arm. *It reminds me of the one in the dentist's office, but this one is much bigger.* The mirror behind the light intensified the brightness, like a searchlight in a lighthouse.

"Better to see you with, my dear." Nurse Mattie grinned as she turned the light toward Arnetta. "The doctor had to be able to see to do the debridement and put in the stitches."

"Du-what? What's that?"

"Debride. Oh, sorry. That's a term we use when we mean to clean the wound. You know, like trash is debris? Well, debridement is getting rid of any foreign bodies or trash from the wound. We call that light our evil eye because it helps us see all the evil."

"Ohh, gross. I mean, she's just been through a car crash, that seems a little like a torture chamber. Couldn't you have waited on that?"

"Oh, trust me, you want anything out of there as soon as possible; otherwise, you'd get an infection, and that's just the start of a whole lot of other problems."

While Arnetta studied the girl as if she would be tested on it later, Nurse Mattie continued, "You can let her sleep, or it's OK to talk to her a little. She may not even remember you're here. We've given her a sedative, a pretty strong one. She's going to be pretty sore all over for the next day or two, but her face will likely show swelling and bruises. I'll just leave you with her for now. If you need anything, I'll be down at the desk or around, just ask."

"Thanks." Arnetta smiled over her shoulder as Nurse Mattie lifted the curtain enough to leave the not so private examination room. *What if she wakes up and starts screaming? What do I do then? Now I sort of wish Nurse Mattie would've stayed.*

As if she could read her mind, Nurse Mattie held the curtain back and said as an afterthought, "If she wakes up confused, it's OK. That's normal. Like I said, if you need me, just holler."

Arnetta smiled and turned back to the girl. She stood there for a long minute looking at the girl, half willing her to wake up, the other half hoping she wouldn't. Arnetta spotted a hard-plastic chair in the corner and pulled it up closer to the girl's bed. The chair made a loud scraping sound as she dragged it across the floor, so she stopped dragging midway to glance toward the bed to see if the noise bothered the girl. *Good. Not even a stir. Man, she really is out.* Arnetta sat there. And sat there. And sat there some more. It probably hadn't been more than ten minutes or so, but it felt like an eternity. *Waiting for something or someone can be an enormous waste of time.* She stood up, again causing the chair to scrape, but she didn't check the face of the girl lying in bed because she figured nothing was going to wake her until she was good and ready.

Arnetta noticed a whiteboard on the wall behind the bed. *I didn't see that before.* She got as close as she could without walking around to the other side of the gurney, which was too close to the other curtained wall. The evil-eye lamp and the sheet-covered bed rail was holding her back from getting a close-up look, but she was able to crane herself over the bedrail, then stretch her neck under the lamp. *I don't want to get too close to Brinda girl or whatever her name is. It would be easier if the writing was more legible. Whoever wrote this probably got an F in handwriting.* Arnetta studied the whiteboard.

EXAM# 6
RN: *Mattie Knowles 3p–3a*
Dr. *Christopher*
Patient: *Brinda Barefoot*
Precautions: *FR*

Hmmmph. Brinda Barefoot. Odd name. Wonder if she made it up on the way in the door. And what does FR stand for? Arnetta stared at the whiteboard. She turned the letters FR over and over in her mouth like pebbles in a rock tumbler. *What if it's some kinda code for AIDS?* Arnetta stepped away at the very thought, and when she did, she hit her head on the evil eye lamp. She hit it hard.

91

CHAPTER ELEVEN

"Ouch!" Arnetta said out loud. Really out loud while touching her head and then visually inspecting her fingers to see if she saw blood. *Nope, but dang, what a lick. Ouch!* Looking down at the formally unintroduced Brinda Barefoot, Arnetta felt silly for her little head bump compared to the swollen, stitched girl lying in front of her. *She's probably not much older than me if a day. I feel so bad for her. I wonder what it's like to be a nurse. Do they want to help everyone the same? Or do some patients mean more to them than others?* Arnetta's hand instinctively reached up, but she caught herself and let her arm fall to her side again. I'm not my mother. *What was I thinking? I can't just brush her hair back from her forehead and tell her everything will be OK. I don't even know her for pity's sake, and I sure don't know everything will be OK. People shouldn't tell you everything will be OK if they don't know.*

Arnetta saw movement. First, a couple of eye twitches, then they opened in little slits like she was staring at the sun. *I guess that's as much as they'll budge with her face swelled up. I think it's gotten worse while I've been standing here. OK, here goes, Arnetta.* There was a half whimper, half groan coming from deep inside the girl, but it hardly made it through her parched lips. Then she saw Arnetta looking at her.

"Who are you?" the girl half-whispered as if she were coming out of a dream.

92

"Who, me?" *Well, that was stupid. Yes, of course, me! I'm the only one standing here aren't I?* "My name's Arnetta. I saw you earlier today. I just wanted to come and check on you. You know, to see if you're OK."

"Why?" The girl turned her head as though it may break. She looked all around the room and then back to Arnetta. "What happened? Where am I?" Her eyes held fright like you'd hold a hot potato. "Who are you?" she'd asked again with the emphasis on the who.

"You're in the hospital. You had an accident. My name is Arnetta. We don't really know each other, it's just that..."

The curtain screeched open, and Nurse Mattie entered with, "I thought I heard talking going on in here. Brinda, my name is Mattie, and I'll be taking care of you while you're here in the ER. You're in Landreth Memorial. Today is Monday, January 28th, 1985. You've been here in the emergency room coming up on two hours. It's just about five-forty-five in the afternoon."

Nurse Mattie continued with mundane information that most people without head trauma never even think about, but when she mentioned the time, Arnetta nearly jumped out of her skin. *Oh my gosh! Gummy is going to kill me. I've got to get out of here. I can't just leave her now, though, right? No, I've got to go. I'll have to find out later how's she doing. I'll come back tomorrow. Wonder if she'll still be here, though? It doesn't matter. Let's get going.* "Um, I've got to go. I didn't realize it was getting late, it's almost six o'clock." Turning to the girl, "I hope you're better soon, I'm really sorry about your accident. I'll see you again soon, OK?"

The girl spoke so slowly, it was hard to decipher what she was saying, but then it registered. "Brinda. Brinda Barefoot. That's Brinda with an i."

Oh, great. Now Brinda girl wants to talk. Arnetta smiled at Brinda, "Nice to meet you, Brinda, with an i." Still smiling, Arnetta looked over at the other set of eyes in the room. *Oops.* Nurse Mattie was giving her the evil eye worse than the magnifying mirrored light ever could.

"I thought you said..."

"Sorry I've got to go." Arnetta ducked out of the curtained room before she could finish getting scolded from Nurse Mattie.

Phew! That was close! She was walking fast through the emergency room and bolted through the door into the lobby. She looked over to where she and L.M. had been sitting. He wasn't there. She scanned the whole room. L.M. was nowhere to be found. *Where is he? Did he leave me here? He wouldn't do that, would he?*

The automatic glass entry doors opened, and in waddled L.M. Their eyes met, and Arnetta saw him tap his wrist while giving her a look of concern. She hurried over to him. She gave him a look too and hoped he understood it. *Oh, if you only knew how glad I am to see you.*

"Arnetta, I better be getting you home. You said your grandmother is a bit of a clock watcher."

Arnetta smiled a frantic smile, but a smile nonetheless, "Where were you? You scared me half to death. I thought you had gone off and left me." Looking outside, she saw the skies were turning that dark pink shade just before sunset.

"I was getting the car, come on, it's right out front here. You're not supposed to leave your car unattended in the turn-around, we better hurry."

"Coming. Thank you so much, L.M. I didn't know it was so late until the nurse mentioned it."

"Well, I was just before coming in to get you. I don't want you to get in trouble with your folks. I mean your grandparents. Sorry."

"Thanks, and it's OK. People do that all the time."

As they were leaving the lobby, Arnetta turned around when she heard a commotion. Nurse Mattie was pouring out of the patient area door like spilled milk. Uh oh.

"Arnetta?" Nurse Mattie halted as she spotted Arnetta. "I need you back in here for a minute."

"Yes, Ma'am?" *By the way she's breathing, I'm guessing aerobics isn't her thing.* "I really need to get home, it's later than I thought."

"I have some questions for you."

"Can't it wait until tomorrow?" *I hope L.M. will bring me back tomorrow.* She stole a quick glance to get his reaction. Nothing.

"I just have a couple of quick questions. It won't take too long."

Arnetta let out a big enough breath for Nurse Mattie to see as well as hear, then turned to L.M. Her just-a-minute finger was held up along with a deer-in-the-headlights stare.

L.M. nodded and pointed to the car.

Walking over to Nurse Mattie to hear just a couple of questions was becoming more than she thought as Nurse Mattie led her back through the doors, down the stinky curtained hall and back into Brinda's exam room. *Well, she seems a lot more awake than she did a minute ago. Why is she looking at me like that?*

"Who are you?"

"I told you. I'm Arnetta", *I guess I better give her more. If I can't remember what all I told her earlier, how can I expect her to remember?* "Arnetta Price. I was on Collier Street today; I was about to go to the dentist's office on Main when I heard a crash. I ran over to see what was going on. Sorry about your accident. I just wanted to see if you were all right."

"I bet you are."

"Pardon me?"

"Sorry. I bet you're sorry."

What in the world? Is she mad at me? "What do you mean? Why wouldn't I be? Well, two can play at this game. "I mean, I just came by here to check on you to see if you're OK. You were alone in the car. I mean, geez, if it were me, I'd be glad somebody wanted to come to check on me."

"Why are you lying?"

"L-lying? What are you talking about? I don't know what you mean."

"Yes, you do. You were there today, but you weren't down the street. Why don't you tell the truth? Nobody cares. I don't care. I just want to know why you're lying. What are you hiding?

Arnetta's eyes were darting like she was watching a ping-pong game, back and forth from Brinda to Nurse Mattie. Seeing that both ping and pong were waiting on an answer, her spine straightened in defense mode, and she could feel her fists starting to clench. "Look. I don't know what you're talking about. You're the one with a bump on the head, not me." She turned to Nurse Mattie, then back to Brinda, "Just ask my friend Amy-I was with her, or ask L.M., he's out in the car waiting on me now. He brought me here because I insisted; I wanted to come and check on you. Now, I'm wondering if that was such a good idea."

Nurse Mattie glared at them both, "Well, somebody better start telling the truth. Do I need to have the police officer come in here?" she looked down at her clipboard, "Officer Jones has cause listed at UI. That's under investigation, but I'm sure he would really appreciate it if you two girls would get your story straight. It'd save a whole lot of time and paperwork. So.... what really happened this afternoon?"

"I told you. I was down the street when I heard the crash. I know the man that owns the shop right in front of where it happened. I was worried about my friend, the man that owns the What's New." *OK, well, that last part may have been a little over the top, but...* "When I got there, I saw a blue car had jumped the curb and knocked over a parking meter. L.M., um, the owner of the store was fine. He had come out to see what was going on too, along with half the county. It was so crowded out on the sidewalk; he and I both went back inside his store to talk about what could have happened. We watched the ambulance and tow truck do their thing as the people on the sidewalk started to dwindle."

"Not exactly. You were IN that store the whole time. I saw you. You saw me. You looked right at me. You saw what happened."

Arnetta looked at Nurse Mattie for assurance. *Hey, look into my eyes. Please throw me a lifeline, I'm sinking over here.* She must've received her thought waves loud and clear, because as the caregiver walked over to her patient to check her lacerations, she spoke in a quiet voice to Brinda, "You know, she could be right. You probably need to rest a little. You've just been through a traumatic experience, Brinda. Sometimes, the mind plays tricks on us, especially after something happens like it did today. You probably did see Arnetta through the window of that store, but the timing... the timing is something else. After you rest, it may become clearer, but sometimes people with head trauma only remember in bits and pieces. Your brain is telling you Arnetta was inside the shop when you had the accident, but in reality, it could've been within minutes after the accident."

Brinda brought both of her wrists together, and then in an upward motion, was able to not only stop the nurse from attending to her wounds but pushed Nurse Mattie away at the same time. You could have cut the air with a knife; the tension was so thick. Brinda put her hands up to cover her ears as her head shook from side to side. She was crying.

"Is she going to be OK?"

Nurse Mattie turned to Arnetta. "She's got to be in some terrible pain. Physical as well as mental exhaustion. She needs to rest."

"I'm right here. You don't have to talk about me like I'm not in the same room." Brinda hadn't lifted her head, her hands still close to her ears, her fists drawn tight. Her words were muffled and sounded like they were coming through clenched teeth. "Why won't you believe me? I'm NOT crazy! Why can't you understand?"

Arnetta turned to Nurse Mattie and said, "I think her head may have been hurt more than y'all think." Brinda lifted her head, lowered her hands, and looked at her in disbelief. Arnetta mouthed *I'm sorry.*

I am sorry. I really am, but I've got to get home. I wish I hadn't sounded so mean to her, but I can't take those words back now. "I've really got to go. Brinda, I hope you're better tomorrow." Arnetta turned and sprinted for the door, out through the lobby to safety of the Sunbeam, the name L.M. had given his car.

"What was that all about, Arnetta?" L.M. was turning the key in the ignition in his black BMW. *It's so weird for a grown man to name his car. Well, grown man is still debatable, but...Hey what is that? I didn't notice that on the ride over here. His foot pedals are weird. Both the gas and brake pedals were about six inches thick. Huh, custom made just for little people.* It registered he was asking a question.

"Pardon?"

"You look spooked. What did the nurse want?"

Arnetta was trying to get buckled in as L.M. was leaving the porte-cochere, "Oh, yeah. I guess I am. Spooked, that is. I'm spooked about a lot of things right now."

"Oh, really? Like what?"

"Well, for one, I'm spooked bout what Gummy's going to say when I drive up in a stranger's car." Out of the corner of her eye, she saw him open his mouth to say something, but she stopped him by continuing, "I'm spooked about that girl. Brinda is her name. Brinda with an i. I'm spooked because she swears she saw me looking at her through the glass storefront of your store. Not after the accident like today, but as the accident was happening. L.M., she saw me looking at her at the same time she was knocking that parking meter over with her car. And I'm spooked because I think you know more than you're telling me. About the mirror." Arnetta turned within the confines of her seat belt and faced L.M. "L.M. that day I walked into your store last Thursday, had you ever laid eyes on me before?"

Nothing from L.M.

"Well?"

He glanced at her a couple of times while keeping his eyes on the road. "Oh, I can speak now?" She could tell he was serious as a heart attack. She could tell because he had raised one of his bushy eyebrows making his face distorted like a paisley painting. *Paisley makes me think of amoebas, and amoebas make me think of my science homework. Focus Arnetta. One thing at a time.* Arnetta was still studying his face waiting on his response. The ride home wouldn't allow time for an extended answer, but she was hoping for some kind of answer. Any answer at all.

L.M. took a deep breath. "First of all, what do you mean, stranger? You told me you OK'd this field trip with your pa..grandparents. Second, Brinda must be mistaken about seeing you as she almost ran into my front window. She's confused, that's all. And thirdly, I resent the insinuation you think I have an ulterior motive here. I had never seen you before the day you seemed to fall out of the sky and into my store. Why would I do that? And the mirror? Well, I admit, I'm not so sure about that mirror, Arnetta."

"What do you mean, you're not so sure?"

"Wait, first things first. What about your grandmother not knowing where you are? We have to be honest and stay honest, Arnetta, there's no other way if you and I are going to be friends. You are a young woman, and the operative word here is young. You're just a child in the law's eyes. I am a business owner. I have a responsibility to be honest and upfront with the public, and I want it to be known the other way around too. All it takes is for one stupid mistake on either of our parts for our friendship to be taken the wrong way."

Arnetta dropped her head a little. She was hurt. She had never even considered anyone thinking it was strange for her to have a friend old enough to be her grandfather, let alone her father, but that's sort of the role Arnetta had put on their friendship. *I guess that makes it hurt more than anything. It's like he's scolding me and threatening to end our friendship.*

"Sorry, L.M., I didn't tell her. I will, though, tonight at dinner. I promise." Arnetta peeked up at him through her bangs, "Would it be all right if, just this once, if you drop me off at the corner near my house? I promise it won't happen again."

"It's against my better judgment, Arnetta."

The silence in the car felt like a crack in a paved road during an earthquake, the underground shifts causing the gap to become bigger and bigger. Eventually, there would be a bottomless abyss, the point of no return.

"OK, Arnetta, just this once. You understand the word once, right? No secrets. I mean it."

Saved! "Ok, Ok. I get it. Thanks. Now, the rest, please?"

"You do not give up, do you? We don't have time to go into detail right now about that mirror. Let me just say, your experience wasn't the first time someone has seen something weird happen.

The rest of the ride home was quiet, but not in a negative way, it was more of mutual respect for each other's resolve to know more. More about each other, and more about the mirror.

Arnett spotted the familiar Stop N Shop gas station on the corner. "Here. Just let me out here, please. It's not much further from here."

CHAPTER ELEVEN

"You sure?"

"Yep, I'm sure. Thanks."

No one was behind them. L.M. put Sunbeam in Park: he folded his hands in his lap while he waited on Arnetta to exit. She unbuckled her seat belt, reached in the back for her raincoat and backpack, and opened the door.

"If you want to come by the store tomorrow Arnetta, I'll tell you more. Don't lose any sleep over it though, it's not worth it."

Arnetta was out of the car, with her forearm resting on the open-door frame, stooping over to reply, "I'll try, L.M." I don't know if I can come tomorrow or not, I'll just have to wait and see. I'll try. I do want to know more. I've got to know more, and I promise not to worry." She closed the door and watched him drive from the intersection of threats and promises.

12

Food and Confession

As it turned out, Arnetta wasn't in trouble with Gummy and Papaw after all. She got home just in time to sit down for dinner, which was probably the equivalent of stealing home base in a baseball game. Gummy had fixed baked chili and beans. Gummy loved her casseroles and said every time, *"You can cook once and eat thrice,"* and she was right about that, her leftovers always seemed to grow. The chili and bean recipe was a Hamburger Helper knock off that Gummy had figured out from looking at the picture on the front of the box because she didn't much believe in packaged, ready-to-prepare foods. She also didn't like one-pot dinners; thus, another reason the casserole lasted for more than one meal. She'd fixed cornbread with corn mixed in it, and her pineapple salad, which was nothing but a couple of slices of canned pineapple on top of lettuce, topped with a spoonful of Duke's mayonnaise and shredded cheese. Next time, the leftover version may be served over cheese toast with a side of okra and stewed tomatoes.

During supper, Arnetta broke the otherwise silent meal. "Gummy, have you ever had a friend that wasn't your age?"

Gummy took her time to answer the obviously loaded question, "Yes, of course, at work, I suppose. I wouldn't really call most of them friends, but I guess in a way they were. Why do you ask? You have a classmate friend that fell behind a year or two?"

"Oh. No, just wondering." Arnetta got up and refilled everyone's glasses with tea from the always present pitcher in the fridge. Sweet tea in their house was referred to as tea because that's the way tea is made. A gallon at a time with three cups of sugar. The longer it sits, the sweeter it gets, but it never sits more than two days if that. Arnetta sat back down, took a long drink of the syrupy, ice-cold drink. As if it gave her the resolve she'd been waiting for, she picked up her fork and announced, "I've got a new friend. He's old."

A man of few words, Papaw chimed in "He? You mean he like a boyfriend? Just how much old is he? You know, I'm a little bit older than your Gummy. Ain't nothin' wrong with that."

"Little bit, you say?" Gummy was mocking Papaw, but she hadn't taken her eyes off Arnetta.

Uh oh. I better get this conversation rolling; otherwise, Gummy is going to start telling the story of how Papaw robbed the cradle. If I hear that story one more time... "Oh, he's not a boyfriend. It's just a man I met the other day. He's really nice," *bite of chili,* "He has a store downtown," *swallow of tea,* "the other day, remember when it rained so hard? I mean, it was pouring, well, I went inside his store till it passed."

"What kind of store, Arnetta? You know you can't be too careful this day and age. You better watch yourself. Watch yourself real good, because there are crazy people everywhere, just watch the news. Why, we just saw on the five o'clock news where a man out in California just got arrested for killing a bunch of people. The Night Watchman I think they called him."

What does it matter what kind of store he has, Gummy? I don't think...

"Stalker," Papaw interjected.

"What?" Gummy gave him a look.

"The newsman said, Night Stalker. Not Night Watchman."

"Well, whatever you call him, I'm just telling you there are crazy people out there." Gummy brought her napkin from her lap and patted her chili stained lips, "And, then there's that Ted Bunter fella. He fooled everyone he met. He..."

"Bundy." Papaw corrected again.

Man, he's on a roll. Papaw loves to watch the news.

"Oh, that's right. Ted Bundy. I'd just as soon forget him altogether. I hope they hang him in the square till the wind

107

whistles through his bones." *Gummy's pat answer for any evil wrongdoer.*

"Y'all, he's not like that. I think I'd know. Besides, he's different."

"Don't be so sure of yourself, Missy. What do you mean, different?" Gummy hadn't picked her fork up yet.

This is turning into more of a conversation than I'd bargained for, and L.M. wondered why I hadn't told them about him. "He's um, he's little."

Papaw was between bites, but his fork halted as if his words took up too much room in his mouth, "You mean a midget?"

"Papaw, they don't like to be called midgets. It's not nice. *You know, like someone calling you a linthead.* I think if you must call them anything, they just prefer little people. He's got this store on Collier Street with all this old stuff in it," Arnetta paused to let out a small laugh, "I mean old things in it." No one else caught the inside joke, so she continued, "Y'all might like to go there sometime and see all the things he has."

"Honey, I've got enough old stuff here to start my own store, but if he's a friend of yours, I may just have to go in and see him and make sure he's on the up and up. I have a way, you know."

"Yes, Ma'am. I know." Arnetta smiled. *Gummy has always thought she had 'a way' that allowed her to read people.*

After supper and washing and putting away the dishes, Arnetta walked through the living room, stopping at the double recliners to give Gummy and Papaw a quick peck on the cheek. "I'm going on upstairs, lots of homework. Good night."

After she sat down at her desk and opened her Biology book, she stared out towards the window, the sun had set on another day. A day filled with all kinds of emotions and even more questions. She returned her eyes to the page of words before her. I hope I can concentrate. Come on, biology, jump into my head. Keep my mind off Brinda with an i, and that dadgum mirror.

13

The Fugitive

Arnetta slept feverishly. She kept dreaming that terrible dream, the one she'd had since she was eight years old. Even though she hadn't known the details of her family's accident until recently, she knew it had to have been terrible. The days following the accident were a blur. Gummy and Papaw had thought it too traumatic for them to have a formal funeral. *I never blamed them, really. They'd just lost their son and grandson, the grandson named after Papaw. I know the accident was terrible for me and Gummy and Papaw, the ones still living, but nothing like it was for my family. My lost-and-gone-forever family.* They held a memorial service later in Greenwood. The bodies had been cremated, their ashes sealed in brass jars, but the urns weren't present at the memorial service. Arnetta didn't really know about the ashes until her fourteenth birthday. *Thanks, Gummy, another excellent birthday present.* That's the time Gummy had chosen to divulge that right after the accident, she'd rented a safety deposit box, a large one, one big enough to hold the five brass urns. Ever since then, every time Arnetta had one of her nightmares, the end changed.

From day one, Arnetta would see the accident as if she were there. There'd be screaming, crying, loud crashes, and lost stares from her Gram and Granpa Jones, her brother, and her parents. The image was always enough to wake her. She used to wonder why they never visited a cemetery. She'd asked Gummy where her family was buried, but her reply was always the same answer. *Doesn't matter, they're not there anyway,* then she'd lay her hand over her own heart and say *they're in here. They're in here forever.* On the night of Arnetta's fourteenth birthday, she'd had the dream again, but this time the nightmare changed. She'd see their van driving down the road in broad daylight. There were smiles. She'd see each of her family members' faces individually full of loving interaction. Then things changed.

The weather turned dark and stormy, rain and hail pelting against the roof and windows. The van swerved all over the road from side to side, and she could hear screams. She tried to scream, but no sound came from her mouth. Then she saw what others in the driving tomb saw. It was the urns. The urns were more prominent than the van itself and were set up in the middle of the road like bowling pins. The urns had faces on them, with horrorstruck expressions. The back row was Granma and Granpa Jones and her mother, the middle row was her daddy, and James and

111

the front row held one center pin. It was HER! The impact sound of the STRIKE always jolted Arnetta awake, damp with sweat, and her heart would be pounding faster than a freight train.

Arnetta woke up, slumped over her study desk. She'd fallen asleep while studying. Again. Something got her attention, and it wasn't just the dream, as if that wasn't enough. She perked up, dragging the back of her fist over the corner of her mouth to wipe up the drool. Tat. *Yes, there it is again. What was that?* She stood up with dreaded anticipation, making her way to the window. She had a thing about walking up to an uncovered window at night, too many slasher movies. *This is stupid, I'm on the second floor for pity's sake, not many twelve feet tall peeping Toms in the world.* Regardless of the realization of giant peepers, she took the long way around the room to approach the window from the side. When she got almost even with the window, TAT! This time it was louder, and she saw it as it made contact; something had hit the window. She nearly jumped out of her skin, and a squelched yelp escaped from somewhere deep inside. She immediately covered her mouth to stifle it, and any more sounds determined to be heard. *What is going on? Is someone there?* Arnetta scanned the area lit by the dim light coming from the living room below. She spotted the culprit. *Oh. My. Gosh! I don't believe it- am I still dreaming?* Arnetta raised the window and leaned out the extra four-to-six inches the screen would allow. It was Brinda. *She must've come here straight from the hospital.*

"What are you doing? Are you crazy?" Arnetta whispered as loud as she could so as not to arouse suspicion from downstairs. *One time I'm glad they have the TV so loud.*

"Well, thanks for the welcome!" Brinda looked down, then back up towards Arnetta, "Nurse Mattie said I should try to remember the accident. She said I should talk with someone."

"Yeah, but what are you doing *here*?" Arnetta ducked her head back into her room and visually checked to make sure her bedroom door was still closed, and then turned back towards the situation outside.

"Well, you left in such a hurry today. We were right in the middle of our conversation."

"So? I had to get home. Which is where you should be. You need to leave. Now. Before my Gum...my Grandparents know you're here."

Brinda looked down again, stretching her neck from side-to-side, and then looked back up. "Aw, come on Arnetta. I really need to talk with you. My neck is killing me, having to look up there. What say you let me come up there? We can finish the conversation we started."

The hair on the back of Arnetta's neck starting to bristle, she began to close the window, "No. It's too late tonight. You need to go home, Brinda."

"Wait! Please don't leave me out here."

Hands still on the window, Arnetta closed her eyes to think. *I can't believe she's already out of the hospital, but Nurse Mattie said observation could mean any time. Crap! Here goes nothing.* Raising the window as high as it would go, Arnetta unlatched the two hooks and paid close attention to the top of the screen so it wouldn't become unlatched and fall to the porch roof. She pushed the screen out enough to slip one leg through the opening and then the other, and onto the porch roof. She'd done it plenty of times before. Sometimes, she'd come out to gaze at the moon, or to try to figure out the constellations, sometimes just to sit and feel nothing at all. *It usually feels good to step outside of my world for a few minutes. This? I'm not so sure. Out here? I'm the one in charge. This is my world. This is where I come to dream of the one-days, and the what-ifs in this world, and my dreams matter. This is different. She's in my space, and something tells me I'm not in my world, and I'm not in charge.* Arnetta thought back to all the times she'd stayed on the porch roof long enough that her clothes would be wet with dew, and that time she thought she'd surely die when she had drifted off to sleep while sitting up with her arms around her knees. She had started to tilt too far over to one side and caught herself but became dizzy and started to fall. That was when she realized her corner of the house had a very sturdy arbor attached to the porch and the roof.

"Geez, Arnetta. I had it pictured another way. Like me inside, not you outside."

"Well, I guess you had it pictured wrong, didn't you?" Arnetta was climbing down the ivy-covered arbor. She jumped the last two feet. "Now what? What do you want?" dusting her hands and walking towards Brinda, she noticed the girl's condition. "Hey, are you sure you're OK? You don't look so good. Your face is oozing a little right there." Arnetta had started to point to the affected area.

Brinda ducked her head back out of reach. "Yeah, I'm good. Hey, listen, I don't know the real reason you left in such a hurry, but I'm glad I found you."

"How did you find me, anyway?"

"That visitor form you filled out had your address on it, it wasn't that hard."

The front screen door opened with a creak like it always did. "Who's out there? Arnetta? Is that you? *Caught by Gummy. A fate worse than death.* Arnetta turned back towards the house just as the porch light came on. "Yes, Ma'am. It's me. It's just me."

"Well, what on earth are you doing out here? It's late."

"Just getting some fresh air, Gummy. I'll be back in in a minute, OK?"

"Well, there's a chill in the air, don't be too long. Who were you talking to? Somebody else out here too?" Gummy used her hand to shield the porch light from hindering her night vision.

OK, well, there you go. I guess it's time to tell Gummy about Brinda, and more about L.M. I really don't want to go into all this tonight. I've got to figure out what's going on myself before I bring them into it. OK, just one little white lie. "A friend from school, Gummy." Arnetta turned to Brinda to introduce her, "This is...." Brinda had vanished. *She's gone.* But where? Arnetta looked around, she hadn't seen or heard anything, but then she noticed a branch of the dogwood tree move as if the wind had blown it, but there was no wind.

"Arnetta?" Gummy let the screen door slam and walked out onto the edge of the porch. "Arnetta? Are you OK?" The rest came out in mumbles, but Arnetta heard her, "I hope you're not sleepwalking. You'd think a normal person would use the door to go outside, that's what they're for."

"Yes, Ma'am. Guess I've been out here long enough tonight. I'm tired, think I'll go on to bed this time. I was studying, and then I fell asleep. Guess I just needed some air." *I wish I could tell you I had that dream again, but then again, I've never told you about that dream, or any dreams, the good ones or the bad ones.*

THE FUGITIVE

The next day at school, Arnetta couldn't keep her mind on her schoolwork. She made sure to run into Amy after lunch. Once again, Amy said she'd give her a lift after sixth-period classes. Arnetta had already decided if Amy hadn't said yes, she'd walk to the hospital as she was no stranger to walking, and it gave her time to think, but she'd rather ride and use her time otherwise today.

Amy drove up to the covered main entrance of the hospital. She offered to wait for a while, but Arnetta told her to go on. She told Amy she was going to see about volunteering to be a candy striper. *Well, it's not really a white lie, it's a matter of timing. I am going to ask about volunteering here, only not today.* Arnetta thanked Amy, and as she drove away, waved with her right hand while her left hand was behind her back with fingers crossed, just to be sure. She entered the double doors, walked up to the main lobby information desk, and asked for directions to the emergency room. *It's so easy to get turned around, all the entrances look about the same, although this entrance seems a little nicer.*

This is going to be a long shot, but I have to try. Arnetta wanted to get Brinda's address from Nurse Mattie. *I've got to find out why she disappeared from my yard last night.* Finding out the nurse she wanted was off didn't help. *Of course, she's off, the story of my life, this is going to take more work than I thought.*

"Oh, I see." Making a story up as she spoke, "Well, I was here last evening. You see, I'm a friend of Brinda Barefoot, and the nurse, Mattie? Well, she called and wanted me to confirm Brinda's address. Said she needed to clarify the records or something."

"Well, you're in luck. We've been busy down here today, normally we would've already taken yesterday's files up to medical records, but they're still over there in that pile that keeps getting taller. Let me look, it shouldn't take long." The workstation attendant flipped through the stack of papers, "Now, what's the patient's name again? Barefoot? Oh yeah, here it is...but wait," the clerk had a furrowed brow as she read scribbled notes. "There's no address showing here for the patient, I'm sorry, I can't remember, what did you say your name is?"

Arnetta forced a smile. I *didn't give you my name, but oh well, here goes nothing.* "Arnetta. I filled out a visitor form yesterday afternoon."

"Oh, so you did, here it is right here. We have your address and phone number, but not one for the patient. Hmmm, now that's just strange." She continued to scan the page, "Oh gosh, we had a runner."

"A what?" Arnetta felt the hairs on her neck stand at attention. She wasn't sure why until the clerk replied."

"A runner, you know AMA."

"I'm sorry...I don't unders..."

"Oh, sorry. Hospital talk. Your friend left without checking out. Do you know where she is? She needs to get herself back here to be checked by the doctor. That must be why Mattie called you."

Oh crap. I think I'm going to be sick. Oh, what tangled webs we weave...how long will it take for them to know Nurse Mattie didn't call me. Think Arnetta. Think. "No, Ma'am, I don't know where she is." Well, at least that much is true. "Maybe her parents came? Maybe they came and took her home? Could that have happened? You know, like you said, y'all were busy, maybe they just walked out."

"No, don't think so. Everybody that comes in here has to fill out the form, just like you did. You were the only one that came back here. Says here, the patient listed her parents as emergency contacts, though. Mr. and Mrs. Les Childs. Wait a minute...she listed her father's name as Les Childs and her mother's name as Hope Childs. Give me a break! Why didn't anybody catch that last night? Your friend pulled one over on us, looks like to me anyway."

"Ma'am?

The clerk looked at Arnetta as if she were the one playing a trick on her. "You don't get it? Sure, you do. Did y'all hatch this plan all by yourselves?" she had gotten the attention of a nurse walking behind the check-in desk.

"What's going on?" the nurse asked as she looked back and forth from the clerk to Arnetta.

"We had a runner last night. Checked in as Brinda Barefoot. Gave her parent's name as emergency contacts. Her parents' names are Hope and Les Childs. Get it?" The nurse grabbed the chart as she mumbled something about the clerk watching too many soap operas. The clerk kept on, "Get it? Hopeless Child? That's what I'm getting anyway."

Arnetta saw the light bulb go off in the nurse's head, it happened to be the same time she got it too. She pursed her lips to keep from smiling. *Hey, I might just get along with this girl, Brinda. If that's even her real name.* The nurse brought her back to reality, "You know what? You should stay here a minute; security may want to talk with you about your friend."

Arnetta couldn't move. Her brain was throwing flaming torches at her frozen body. *Get out of here. Get out of here now. You don't know what you're getting into. Just leave.* The ice statue of the nice Arnetta won out. "OK. I'll wait." Arnetta remembered the information behind Brinda's emergency room bed. *Now, I understand what the FR stood for. Flight risk. I hope I'm doing the right thing here. Who is Brinda? Why would she run?* As soon as the clerk left, Arnetta's body melted, and she high tailed it out the door. *Great! That's stupid, they may not have Brinda's address, but they sure as heck have mine!*

Arnetta nearly dove into the What's New shop for the second time in less than a week. L.M. was talking with a customer, so she pretended to be looking at a display of items near his work desk. Finally, after what seemed like an eternity, he was by himself.

"L.M. I think we have a problem."

"We?"

"Yes, we. Me, you and Brinda. And the mirror."

L.M. sat down in a Queen Anne winged armchair. "Not that again."

"Yes that." Arnetta plopped down in a matching chair across from L.M. but pulled herself up to sit on the edge. She held onto the arms of the chair as if to hold herself down. "And that's not all."

"Oh, pray, tell. There's more?"

"Yes. I think the police might be looking for me."

"What?" L.M. stiffened up, "What have you done?"

"Me? I haven't done anything. It's Brinda."

"Well, what has *she* done then?"

"I don't know if she's done anything...yet. But she's missing. She left the hospital last night without checking out. I mean, she just up and left. Like I'm outta here...gone. L.M. she's a fugitive."

L.M. was silent, his eyes seem to be searching for an answer.

"As I said, I don't know why she ran, but it looks like I'm the only real contact person the hospital has right now. I'm scared, L.M. What am I going to do?" Not waiting for a reply, Arnetta rose and walked to the door. Her hand on the doorknob, she turned back toward L.M., who was getting up as well. "I've got to go home. I'll be back tomorrow." She shook her head, "No, wait a minute. I promised to babysit tomorrow. I'll be back the day after tomorrow, L.M., and when I come back, I want you to tell me everything you know about that mirror. Please, I have to know. I don't want just to know, I need to understand, but I don't have time today. Besides, between this Brinda thing, the hospital is looking...and well, I just don't have time. See ya." and with that, a determined Arnetta was out of the door, hurrying down the street towards home.

14

Power of Reflection

That night, Arnetta had a hard time trying to get to sleep. Her thoughts kept going back and forth between Brinda and L.M. First, there was Brinda. *Where is she? WHO is she? Why did she run from the hospital? Why did she come to see me, here of all places? The questions are floating around in my brain like balls of mercury that just keep multiplying when they bump into each other. She scares me a little, but in an intriguing way. I can't put my finger on it, but I think I really want to get to know her. Then, there's L.M. I mean, isn't it just a little weird that I'd never seen him before? This isn't a big town at all, so why haven't I seen him at the grocery store, the gas station, on the street, anywhere? He's someone I would've noticed for sure, but I hadn't laid eyes on him before I'd wandered into the What's New shop. Besides the rain, I'm beginning to think there was some other reason I went into that store last week. And the mirror that showed me the accident? What is that all about? L.M. hadn't seemed all that concerned about the wreck I saw or thought I saw, no...I did* see it, and then it happened! When I saw the accident *in the mirror, it was as if time had stopped. It was definitely Brinda in that blue car. I'll never forget the look on her face as the wreck was happening, it was a wordless conversation that never took place, yet it seemed to last forever. And, when I met her 'for the first time' in the hospital, I think she and I both knew exactly when we'd actually first met, but neither of us would talk about it because it just doesn't make any sense. Maybe that's why she came to my house, but why did she leave?*

Arnetta reached over to hit the snooze button on her alarm clock radio. She had set it to come on early and loud, and a Tears for Fears song was playing, and it was doing the trick. The beat of the song helped her lift her head from the soft pillow, throw the covers back and plop both feet on the braided rug by her bed. After she dressed, Arnetta packed her backpack with a few extra things since she'd be going straight to babysit after school. She adored Benjamin Wood. Even though Benji had plenty of his own books, Arnetta liked taking a couple of her favorites to share with him. He was an only child, and his parents really spoiled him rotten. *Mr. and Mrs. Wood reminds me of Mama and Daddy, I guess so anyway. They make me laugh at their corny jokes, look at each other when they talk, and you can tell they think the world spins around little Benji. His out-of-control blonde hair framed his chubby face, and his little cheeks looked like ripe apples. Hard to believe he'll be four next week.* The Woods always liked Arnetta to come a few minutes

124

early so they could give her their instructions. *Even though I've babysat for them plenty of times, sometimes they act like I don't know what to do. They pay well, though. $1.50 an hour, and Mr. Wood usually tips me when he drops me off at home. I'm not complaining.*

Another reason she liked going to their neighborhood is that it was in a subdivision. The houses were just as close together as her neighborhood, but the difference was like night and day between Holly Hill and her own 'mill hill.' Babysitting in Holly Hill Subdivision last summer is where she'd first met Craig Walker. His family moving to Landreth the week before was perfect timing for Arnetta, as he hadn't had a chance to be prejudiced by all the other kids at school yet. It had been a long hot summer day, so Arnetta was in the Wood's backyard playing with Benji in his little wading pool. Benji's laughter as he splashed in the shallow water made her laugh too, but it wasn't the only sound she heard. There was a noise behind her that was both mesmerizing and annoying at the same time. It was the rhythmic sound of a basketball bouncing on the pavement. Then it stopped. Feeling that familiar prickle on the back on her neck, she turned around and there he was, the most beautiful guy she's ever seen. She forced a quick smile and turned back to Benji. *Arnetta, the sun must be getting to you! Who is that? And where did he come from?* She looked down at her cut-off blue jean shorts and almost white sleeveless blouse. *Well, it's not the worst babysitting clothes I could've worn, I guess.*

"Hi."

Her ponytail flew when she turned her head in response. *Is he talking to me? It's so hot out here, his words are melting like butter. Well, word. It was just one word. Of course, he's talking to, I'm the only one here. Oh no, awkward silence.* The heat rushing to her cheeks would be a dead giveaway. *The sun! Yes, thank you for the sun, I'll blame my blush on the sun.* Arnetta stood and brushed off the seat of her pants.

"Hello. Are you the new neighbor?" *Dumb question, Arnetta. Of course, he's the new neighbor. Why else would he be playing basketball in the driveway of the house that's been empty for a month?* "I'm Arnetta, and this..." walking around to the back of the little pool to keep a better eye on her charge, "This is Benji."

"I'm Craig. Yeah, new neighbor." He was standing there, just looking all hunky, volleying the basketball from hand-to-hand, then pointed to Benji. "Cute kid. You have any *older* brothers?"

Arnetta looked from Craig to Benji, then back to Craig, "Oh, no. This is...he's not...I mean, I'm Arnetta...the baby-sitter. I don't live here. Benji doesn't have any brothers or sisters."

"Oh." He looked down at his basketball and lifted it with one hand as an explanation. "Sorry about that. Where do you live?"

"Oh, I live...across town a bit." Arnetta leaned over and patted Benji's back softly, checking to be sure he wasn't getting sunburned while taking time to change the subject. "You like basketball? Our school has a pretty good team. You'll be meeting them soon enough when the session starts in a few weeks." *And that will be the end of you talking to me.* "We only have one high school, you know."

"Yeah, I heard. Do you like school here?"

"Yeah. I guess." *No one has ever asked me that before.* "I mean, I guess it's just about as good as any."

"Well, I'll let you get back to...your job." Instead of leaving, he just stood there looking at her.

"Ok," *And you can get back to your solo game.* "Well, nice meeting you." *His eyes were so blue. His hair was a sun-kissed, golden blonde. If I didn't know any better, I'd swear he's Sonny Crockett's little brother. A little Don Johnson. This guy could very well be on Miami Vice, one of my favorite shows.*

"You too. See you 'round." He turned and bounced the ball a few more times, hit a ringer, but the next time Arnetta looked away from Benji, Craig Walker had disappeared.

She had seen him a couple of more times in passing, but not until school started and they were assigned lab partners had they said more than a few words to one another. She

127

figured he'd been schooled by the other guys that she was off-limits. It's not that the other kids were ever mean to her, but they never included her in their circle of friends.

Today was different. Here sat Arnetta and Craig at the same lab table, near the back of the room, Mrs. Griffin busy tapping out her chalkboard assignments, Craig leaned over towards her and whispered.

"Whatcha been up to lately, Arnetta?"

"Oh, nothing much."

"Just wondering, cuz I haven't seen you over at the neighbor's house in a long time."

"Yeah, it has been quite a while. The Woods went on a cruise and then off in their Airstream for about three weeks."

"Must be nice, huh?"

"Yeah, tell me about it."

"Funny, you should ask, though."

"Yeah? Why's that?"

"Cuz, I'm babysitting this afternoon, right after school."

"Oh yeah? Need a ride?"

Mrs. Griffin had finished and turned around to the class. Arnetta mouthed 'maybe' to Craig, and he nodded. Her teacher was a stickler about paying attention in class, and Arnetta had heard others griping about their punishment of staying after school and copying the Dictionary for an hour. One guy had even complained to her that it was a waste of time, and she gave him another day of detention. He said he never got past aardvark, but that didn't seem to matter to Mrs. Griffin.

Maybe? Good one, Arnetta. Should I? It's not too far to walk. I was going to ask Amy if it was raining, and it's not. I mean, he does live right next door to where I'm going. Arnetta mulled her response while listening to Mrs. Griffin compare the genetics of vegetables and people, and while pretending to jot class notes, she slid a small piece of paper over to Craig. He glanced down to see two words: Sure. Thanks.

He smiled, picked up his pen, and while looking at Mrs. Griffin, he drew a smiley face on the paper. Arnetta melted a little inside. *Ok, so what if it was a Picasso version, it's the thought that counts, right?*

While gathering their belongings after class, they had a chance to use real words instead of notes and strained whispers. "OK, well, see you after school. You know my car, right?"

"Yeah." *Oh no. Too quick. No, no, no.* "I mean, yeah, it's red and black, right? I think I saw you drive it up to your house last time I was at the Woods." *I see that smile. He knows. He knows I've been watching him.*

When she got to his car, there was no place to sit. She had to wait for him to maneuver some things around to make room. He tossed his book bag in the back floorboard, but his car phone had to be handled with a little more care. *Wow! A car phone! I wish I had someone to call so I can say I used it.* The handle at the top of the leather-like bag made it easier to lift, but the touch-tone dial-and-talk part kept falling out, trailing the thick, long coiled cord. It was all attached to the essential part of the phone, the battery. Craig apologized the whole time he was fiddling around with it, "I'm sorry. My mom got me a phone, so I could call her in case of an emergency. So far, the only emergency has been for me to stop by the store to pick up mayonnaise and stuff like that."

Arnetta laughed, "Oh, but that's sweet, and look how much time it saves."

"Yeah, I guess. We've got three phones in our house. And an intercom. My dad teases her all the time and tells her he's going to invent a phone she can keep in her pocketbook, so she won't ever be without one."

"Ha! Wouldn't that be the day?"

"I know. Can you imagine? It would be like Dick Tracy talking into his wristwatch phone."

They both laughed at the possibility, and then Craig continued, "Well, if we can put a man on the moon...."

Arnetta took in her surroundings. *This is so cool. Craig's late birthday had caused him to be one of the old kids in her class. Already seventeen and has his own car. A car with a phone. And not just any car, a shiny red Mustang with a con-*

vertible top. Yep, he's quite the catch. The game of catch. That's one game I don't play. I wish someone would see me in this car, but then again, I don't want to embarrass him. Arnetta adjusted herself in the seat and buckled her seat belt like a good girl. *I'm just going to enjoy the ride and pretend this is a perfectly ordinary thing to do. Riding in this beautiful car with a cute guy on a beautiful day. Time can stop right now. Please.*

The evening went fast as she had imagined it would. She had Benji fed, bathed, and in bed by seven o'clock, one of his parent's rules. She had at least an hour to kill before the Woods came back, so she turned on their stereo system to listen to some of their cassettes while doing her homework. Arnetta picked up the first case, a Lionel Ritchie tape, but held it as she skimmed the first row of the Woods' immense music collection. *Geez, they've got everything here: Lionel, Madonna, James Taylor, London Philharmonic Orchestra, Dolly Parton, and oh, there's an Etta James album featuring her song, At Last.* She pulled out Etta and returned Lionel to its spot. There's a good chance she never would've heard of Etta James' songs if not for her mother. She played it over and over and imagined her mama and daddy slow dancing over by the corner window.

The Etta James song was still in her head as Mr. Wood dropped her off in front of her house. He handed her a ten and told her to keep the change. *Not bad money for do-*

ing nothing but playing with a cutie bug. Arnetta stuffed the bill into her jeans pocket and walked up the steps to the lit front porch. *Thanks for leaving the light on, Gummy, I'm glad you remembered this time.* She turned and waved to Mr. Wood, signaling she was in and watched him drive off. She recalled a time Gummy had forgotten the front porch lights and had already locked the door for the night, leaving Arnetta no choice but to pound on the door until they finally heard it. Even then, Mr. Wood sat out front with his headlights on until she was safely inside.

It was only nine-thirty, but Gummy and Papaw were already in their bedroom. *Early to bed, early to rise.* When Arnetta reached her room, she closed the door quietly, then tossed her book bag on top of the bed covers at the same time she flicked the lights on.

"Ow!"

Arnetta nearly jumped out of her skin. "What..What are YOU doing here?"

"Keep your voice down, I'm waiting on you, what do you think?" Brinda's eyes were squinting, trying to adjust to the abrupt light in the room as she sat up, stretching her arms upward in a long yawn as she twisted her body, and let her feet reach the floor.

"How did you get up here? Does Gum...my grandmother know you're here? And...you're sleeping on my bed?"

"Settle down Goldilocks. I just needed to talk with you. Did your grandparents see you come in? I didn't know you'd be so long. I couldn't turn on the lights now, could I? This is a comfy bed, isn't it? I guess I fell asleep."

"No, they've gone to bed, why? How did you get in here past them?"

Brinda gave the nod towards the window she'd seen Arnetta crawl out of previously, then added, "Good. Well, in the morning, we can tell them I came home with you from wherever you've been."

"Where I've been is babysitting, if that's any of your business. I can't believe you've been here in my room." Arnetta looked around, "What have you been doing?"

"I told you. Waiting on you. Well, and I took a nap."

"What's your plan? You don't mean you're just going to barge in here and expect to spend the night, do you? That's a little forward, don't you think?"

"Well, we didn't have much time to talk about it, did we? I can't help it you're so late coming home. Pretty late for a school night, isn't it?" Brinda yawned again, "Aren't you tired?"

"I was tired, but for some reason, I'm not anymore. Maybe something about someone being in my room, in my bed!" *I really don't mind the company, I guess. But what a bold move! I'd never do this to anyone, especially to someone I don't even know.* "What about your parents? The people listed on your hospital form? Brinda, I really don't know anything about you. Where do you live?"

"Oh, here and there. Right now, here. I don't mean actually *live* here like you do, but I usually just live where I am. You'd understand if you've been moving around as much as me."

"So, you're in foster care? Where are you supposed to be right now? Is Brinda really your name? Or did you make that up too? And what about Barefoot? Where'd you dream that one up?"

"Thanks, Arnetta." Brinda looked down as she pressed her hand on her knees, then looked back up at Arnetta with genuine hurt in her black eyes. "That's the only real thing about me. It's Cherokee. Well, Barefoot was my grandfather's name."

"Well, how'd you get here then? We're a long way from the reservation. Is that where you're from? The reservation?" Arnetta took a step forward and rested a knee on the corner of the bed.

"Not as far as you'd think. Not as the crow flies anyway. I sort of borrowed the car. You know that old blue car, the Gremlin? Well, it actually belongs to my neighbor's uncle. He's in the hospital somewhere. I think. My neighbor, Joey? He's a little older than me, he's pretty cool, and he knows what I've had to put up with."

"Like what? You mean.... you ran away? You really *are* a fugitive!"

"No, I'm not."

"Yes, you are. You stole a car. You ran away. You left the hospital without them saying it was OK to go, which they're not too happy about, by the way. They were trying to question me! Me of all people."

"Wait, you went back to the hospital?"

"Yes. After you disappeared from here. I...I just had un-answered questions."

"Yeah. Me too. That's why I'm here. Well, sort of."

"Yeah, well, it's the 'sort of' we were getting to a minute ago. So, did you? You know, run away?"

"It's not so bad, really. I had some bad things happen, and my mom either never believed me, or she was afraid of confronting my father, so one day I'd just had enough. That's when...I left. My father...well, my stepfather, drinks a lot with his friends. He's not supposed to drink, but when he does, he turns into a crazy man. He gets abusive. You don't even want to know, and you sure don't want to be around him when his fists start flying. Nothing ever suited him, and everything was always my fault. I guess I just got tired of being his punching bag."

Arnetta went from resting her knee on the corner of the bed to a full seated position facing Brinda. It was a slow movement as if the breath from Brinda's words were deliberately setting her down gently. "Can't you get help? I mean, can't the police make him stop? Won't your mom tell the police what's going on?"

"I live on the reservation. We don't have police; we have tribal elders. They would side with him anyway, and some of them are his drinking buddies. It's OK. I talked with my mom once since I've been gone. I called from a payphone when I got to Traveler's Rest. I think everything will be OK now. She says he's better when I'm not there. I have a younger brother and two little sisters in that house. He's their real father. I'm thinking I did the right thing if it makes it easier on them."

"Brinda, I'm so sorry."

"It's OK. Things didn't used to be so bad. Like I said, it's the alcohol. He's always been quick- tempered, and has been known to be mean to others, but never physical until the family got bigger. Well, his family got bigger about the same time he stopped working."

"Did he get hurt at work? On the job?"

"No, I wish. I mean, I shouldn't say it like that. My old man used to be in construction. He could fix anything, but he was good at being a carpenter, but now he can't work. That's when the heavy drinking started. My mom said the meanness started boiling in the bottle.

"I don't get it. Why can't he work then? Is it drinking? Was he drinking on the job?"

"No, they started a new restriction on the reservation. When you build something or add something, you know, like replacing a roof or something, you have to get a building permit, and now, you can't get a building permit unless you have a contractor's license. My dad doesn't have a license, he's just a handyman. He was so sure the people at the Office of Building Code Enforcement had it in for him, he really got paranoid. When you mix paranoia with alcohol, you get trouble. My father couldn't take going from being the man-in-charge to a gopher. Chief Youngblood has been at our house plenty of times trying to keep the peace.

"Sorry, Brinda. I had no idea. I'm so sorry. Your poor mama. I can't imagine...Oh, I didn't let you finish telling me about the car. Oh, my gosh Brinda, you *were* driving a stolen car, weren't you?"

"Not stolen, borrowed. There's a difference. Remember, I told you about my neighbor? I'm sure Joey would back me up. He told me his uncle had already been in the hospital for over a month, and it wasn't looking too good for him to be released. I hate hospitals. Anyway, Joey would go out and crank up the Gremlin once a week and let it run about five minutes to keep it from getting all stoved up."

"I'm glad you let your mama know sort of where you are. Do you need to call her now? We can go to the payphone in town. Gummy would probably have a conniption fit to see a long-distance call on her bill, and to the reservation at that."

"No. I've called her once. She knows I'm OK."

"But..."

"She's not technically my mom. My real mama died giving birth to me sixteen years ago. She's really my aunt. So, I've always called her Mom. She got married to 'him' when I was ten and started having her 'own' children. I never knew who my real dad was and was completely happy when it was just my mom and me. I love my brother and sisters, but I guess I really resented being the babysitter. When money got really tight, he yelled at my mom, and I'd yell at him, and that's when I found out you don't yell at him. I guess I'm just bad news all the way around." Brinda's shoulders slumped a little lower. "I hate it about the car. I mean, Joey told me I could borrow it if I ever really needed to, you know, escape. He said to take it as long as you need it. I don't think he meant forever, and I reckon he would've liked for me to return it in one piece." She turned to Arnetta, and it seemed her remorse turned to anger like a flick of a switch. "Piece of crap. A death trap! That car almost killed me! Damn brakes. I was lucky that the parking meter was there, or I would've gone right through that plate glass window! And what if I'd been on the highway?"

The weight of the world pressed the air out of the room, as they both sat in silence. It seemed like forever until

Brinda spoke again, almost in a whisper. "I'm in deep trouble when the cops run the registration on that car. I think Joey said his uncle never had it put in his name. He won it in a card game, and the man died before they ever got it transferred."

Arnetta shook her head. "Oh man, this just keeps getting worse, Brinda. But how did you get here? To Landreth? Why, Landreth?"

"This town is close enough to the mountains, and it reminds me a little bit of home. Home. That's a funny word for me. It's only been about a week since I left the reservation, but I've sort of been on my own since I was about ten, since my brother and sisters started coming along. Even though I was living there, I just sort of tried to stay out of the way. I did my part to help take care of the babies, went to school, and kept to myself. In the car, I saw the name Landreth on the map, and for some reason, I felt drawn to it. The map I had showed Highway 11 close by as the Cherokee scenic highway. Apparently, the Cherokee used to use it long before it became a highway."

"But where are you staying?"

"I'm living in.... well, was staying in my car. It's now in the custody of the police. So...I guess I don't have a place to stay."

"I've seen pictures of homeless people on TV, but you sure don't look like them. I mean, you look normal. I mean, you look just like anybody else."

"I am anybody else, Arnetta. I'm no different than you. Not really."

Arnetta felt like a hole was burning in the pit of her stomach. Her hands were in her lap, her balled fists looked like they were ready for a fight. A fight with her inner self. She remembered something Gummy told her many times, especially when she was feeling sorry for herself. *"Arnetta, there's always going to be people that are better off than you, but just you remember, there's always going to be people that are worse off than you too. Plenty worse off." When Gummy told me that, I couldn't imagine someone being worse off than me, and here I sit, looking straight into the deep, dark eyes of misfortune.*

After another minute, Arnetta broke the silence, "Well, it's getting late. If you're staying tonight, we'd better get some sleep."

Arnetta made a pallet on the floor for Brinda. She pulled an old sleeping bag out of the closet for a makeshift mattress and a blanket for cover. On top of the braided rug, the temporary bed wasn't too bad, a whole lot better than the back seat of a Gremlin. "Sorry about the floor, but some nights, I think my twin bed isn't even big enough for me." Arnetta laughed as she went to her dresser to get her pajamas, but something caught her eye. When she turned around, she noticed Brinda already sliding into her new bed on the floor.

"What are you doing? Aren't you going to change first?"

"I pack light, Arnetta, in case you haven't noticed."

Arnetta, motionless and speechless, stared down at Brinda, then saw Brinda's clothes neatly stacked beside the sleeping bag. The look in Arnetta's eyes must have said enough.

"I mean, I really do pack light, and it's getting lighter all the time. Everything I have is in the car, and who knows where that is. It's OK, Arnetta."

"No, it's not. It's not OK. Get up, I've got some things you can borrow." *She's about my size, I guess. She may not like my style, whatever that is, but beggars can't be choosers.*

"You don't have...."

"I know I don't have to, but I am, and don't you think a thing about it either. Believe me, it's no big deal. It's not like what I have is all that great anyway."

Arnetta pulled out a fresh pair of pajamas, panties, and then "Um, what's your bra size? Think you can wear any of these?" Arnetta kept digging in the recesses of her dresser, "While I'm at it, here are some other things you can try on. You can wait until in the morning if you want." She'd pulled out a pair of black faded jeans, a long sleeve red t-shirt, and a couple of other shirts.

"Good god, you're a regular J.C. Penney, aren't you? Thanks! I mean it. I'll check 'em out in the morning. I'm good for the night."

"Like I said, not a big deal. We don't have a bathroom up here, sorta crappy, but that's just how it is. My room used to be the attic, but I like it up here. It's like I have a place of my own. In a way."

Brinda turned around and took in the whole room. "Man, you've got it made, and you don't even know it. At my house, me and my two little sisters and brother all shared one bedroom, and it wasn't near the size of this space. Now that's togetherness." Brinda looked over towards the window and into the darkness. "I wonder if they miss me."

"I'm sure they do. Hey, listen, Gummy and Papaw get up early, so if you want to get in and out of the bathroom without causing a scene, you'll want to get downstairs before six. The towels and washcloths are inside the bathroom, in the linen closet. Wrap your hair in a turban, that way if one of them sees you, they'll probably think it's me." Arnetta stopped talking and walked over to the window, and without turning around, she continued, "It's not that I'm trying to keep you a secret or anything. There's just no sense in getting into anything before school, that's all, or else we'll never get out of the door."

They talked long into the night after the lights were out, chatting about anything and everything. *I think I've met my new best friend. Quite possibly the only best friend I've ever had.* They'd decided that right after school, they'd go to the What's New shop so L.M. could meet Brinda. To say Brinda's curiosity was piqued regarding L.M. and the mirror would be an understatement. Arnetta tried to explain her new friendship with the little man and the mirror, but no amount of explaining could tell the real story. *I'll simply have to show her. It's a mystery to me too.*

The pauses in their conversations clued them both in; it was time to call it a night. "Well, goodnight Brinda. See you in the morning." The only response was "hmmm," letting her know Brinda was already more than halfway to dreamland. Arnetta smiled to herself. A smile that allowed her to know all was right with the world. Well, for tonight anyway. *I guess we're in this together. That's nice.* That's the last thing she remembered before the sandman washed over her mind with slumber like new, foamy water replacing the retreating tide at the beach.

Both girls walked toward the high school, and the last intersection before, Brinda turned to Arnetta. "OK, here's the deal. I know I told you last night I'd go to school with you, but I've been thinking that's not such a good idea."

"Why not? We talked about this. You're visiting me and monitoring my classes. What else are you going to be doing all day?"

"Well, for one thing, the police might be asking questions, and a good place for them to start would be at school, don't cha think?"

"OK. I guess you're right, but what *will* you do?"

"I don't know. I may just go on to that store you're talking about. I could just hang out there until you get out of school."

Arnetta's face flushed a little. *Slap! Well, it may as well have been. Am I jealous? That's stupid, but how dare Brinda try to jump my introductions. I'm not sure if I should shield L.M. from Brinda, or the other way around. I must've said too much last night. Here goes nothing.* "Brinda, don't be stupid. That's a crazy idea. He's working. You might get in his way."

"What's the matter, Arnetta?" Brinda used a teasing, childish whine, "I'm not good enough for your new little friend? Think I can't handle your little secret mirror?"

"No. That's not it." Pushing her glasses up as far as they'd go, smashing against her forehead, "No, it's not that at all." Arnetta turned away from Brinda to continue the walk to school. Turning her head over her shoulder, she continued, "Do what you want to do Brinda, I don't care. Just remember, though...Oh, forget it." *What's the use? Telling her not to hurt L.M. makes him sound like a child, and her a monster. My stomach is in a knot. The third wheel, that's it. I'm going to be like that third wheel. But there's got to be a reason that mirror brought the three of us together. I could skip school... No, wrong choice. I'll just have to trust my gut. Trust my gut and trust Brinda and trust L.M. not to shut me out.*

15

Craig

Arnetta had a terrible time keeping her mind on school. It didn't help that she kept running into Craig. Since the beginning of the school year, they'd been friendly to one another in the hallway. They'd always spoken to each other, but on occasion, they'd hang out a couple of minutes while one or the other retrieved something from their locker. After Mrs. Griffin assigned them together as lab partners, things had begun to change. At first, Arnetta didn't put much into it. *What's up with Craig? Is it me, or is he really looking at me more these days? Not just looking at me, more like looking through me.* Arnetta had started paying a little more attention to what she was wearing, especially on lab days when she had sit more closely to Craig. She wasn't one for wearing much makeup, not like some of the girls, but she'd started re-applying lip gloss throughout the day, and had added a little mascara to her light-brown lashes. Maybe an extra-slow step underneath the mist of her favorite perfume, Sweet Honesty, in the mornings. *I hope Craig doesn't think I'm doing all that for him. Does he? Am I?*

Today, during Biology class, he seemed to be sitting a little closer than usual, and a lot closer than necessary. Well, it is easier to share the microscope this way. Sitting closer meant contact. I'm not sure if he notices or not, but his left knee keeps brushing against my right leg, and what do I do? My reflex is to move my leg over. Every time. Just leave your leg in one place, Arnetta, just to see what he does. He's bound to notice, right? There it is again...Dang it! C'mon leg. Sit. Stay. Oh, I see what's happening here as I observe the smirk on his adorable face. He knows he's getting to me. Biology. Stop it Arnetta, pay attention to Mrs. Griffin.

"What's the matter with you today?" he'd had the nerve to whisper about half-way through class.

"Me? Up with me? Nothing, why?" She'd answered him by looking down into her Biology book, so as not to alert the teacher.

"I don't know, you just seem a little jumpy, that's all."

You think? If you had a hunk rubbing up against... "Oh, it's nothing. I didn't get much sleep last night. I guess my brain is on hyper-alert, but I'm not. I'm just sleepy."

Craig held an imaginary item in his hand and hoarsely whispered in a fake TV commercial voice, "Is the anatomy of amoebas keeping you awake at night? Try new, improved Amoeba Osmosis, guaranteed to transfer biology knowledge into your head automatically while you sleep. Order now, and we'll include the book, The Wonderful World of Pond Scum, absolutely free. But wait, there's more...."

Arnetta couldn't help it. She laughed out loud. Really loud. As soon as she realized, she covered her mouth, but it was too late, Mrs. Griffin had stopped talking and was looking straight at her over the top of her dark-rimmed glasses.

"Arnetta Price! Mind telling me what's so funny back there?"

Everybody turned around. Craig had lowered his hand, the one holding the pretend item he was selling. He'd straightened up and turned towards Arnetta with an utterly somber face as if he had no clue.

"Um, I'm sorry, Mrs. Griffin. I guess it just dawned on me that um, the amoeba sorta resembles some paisley pajamas I used to have. It's kinda gross to think about sleeping with all those amoebas."

The class laughed, but Mrs. Griffin didn't. Craig gave her a *nice save* look.

"Class? Class!" Everyone stopped and turned back towards the front of the room. Mrs. Griffin looked at Arnetta, "Let's save the entertainment portion of Biology class until after the bell rings, shall we?"

"Yes, Ma'am. Sorry."

After class, Craig apologized to Arnetta for making a scene. *It's OK, I didn't mind,* but "Apology accepted," is what she'd answered with a smile. *It's OK, at least it helped me get my mind off L.M., Brinda, and that mirror... for a few minutes, at least.*

They walked together to the last period of the day, and although they didn't share the class, their rooms were right across the hall from each other. It took nearly all the ten minutes allotted between classes to get to them because they were on the opposite ends of the school campus. Luckily, it wasn't raining, so they walked the outside corridor, which meant they could carry on a conversation and a leisurely walk instead of the crowded hallway, sometimes referred to as salmon alley because it felt like salmon fighting to get upstream.

"Craig, did I tell you I met a new girl in town? Well, she's just passing through, but..."

"No, who is she? You have any classes with her?"

"No, like I said, she's just passing through Landreth. She's seventeen, and already done with school."

"She graduated early? Cool. I've thought about graduating early too, but, according to my mom, I should've already done something about it. She's talked me into staying the whole twelve years. Said if I wanted to skip a grade, it should've been the 11th, not the 12th. I guess she's right, who wants to skip their senior year?"

"She didn't finish school, Craig. I said she's *done* with school."

CHAPTER FIFTEEN

"She's a drop-out, Arnetta?" Craig stopped and looked at Arnetta like she was from Mars. "Where'd you meet a loser like that?"

"Don't say that! You're just being a dweeb, Craig. You don't even know her. She's had some problems, but she's working them out. I think. Anyway, she's OK. You should meet her." *Are you crazy, Arnetta?* "Or...maybe not. I mean, she's just going to be here another few days or so." *If I only knew what Brinda was thinking. Is she here for just a few days? Is she planning on settling here in Landreth? Some people are as easy to read as an open book, and the ending is kind of pre-dictable. You may not know the ins and outs of their daily life, but their path is usually obvious. Like me, for example, I'll graduate next year, get a part-time job, and go to Tri-County or Southwestern Community College, hopefully transferring to a four-year. I'll probably major in early education and stay here and teach or something.*

"Hellooo."

"What? Oh sorry. I was deep in thought."

"Whatever. I was saying I'm sorry. I guess I shouldn't have been so quick to judge. You know, that old walk a mile in my shoes thing."

"Huh?"

"You know, the old Indian saying, until you walk a mile in my shoes, you will never know what I've been through. It's something my mom says all the time."

"That's so weird."

"What, you've never heard that saying before?"

"No. I mean yeah, I've heard it, sure. It's just funny you should pick *that* saying though. Brinda is an Indian."

"Oh, cowboy and Indian Indian? Or you know, like from India, a real Indian?"

Arnetta playfully swatted Craig's arm. "You're being a dweeb again. Knock it off. American Indian."

Slowing their walk as they approached their classroom, Craig stopped and turned to Arnetta. "Hey, I wanted to ask you something, but it can wait. What are you doing after school?"

Uh oh. Here it comes. Me and my big mouth. Craig is going to ask me to introduce him to Brinda. Should've known. "Me? Um, nothing really, I guess. I've gotta go see a friend downtown, why?"

"I can take you if you want me to. Like I said, I wanted to talk to you a little anyway."

"Sure, see you then."

They both turned into their respective classrooms for the last period of the day. *Hmmm. Wonder what he wants to talk to me about? Is it Brinda? Does he want to ask me out? Yeah, fat chance, Arnetta. I bet he wants me to help with his Biology paper. That's it. He wants a Tutor!* Satisfied she had solved her mystery question; she was able to pay better attention in her political science class for the next hour.

16

The Invitation

Arnetta could hear the Mustang before she spotted the red car with Craig inside. He had already settled in the idling car, and the bass sounds were thumping as loud as someone trying to get out of a trunk somewhere.

"Are you deaf?" *Apparently, you are, or soon will be.* Craig was still drumming his steering wheel and bobbing his head to the beat. Arnetta tapped on the window. Nothing. She knocked a little harder. Nothing. *Great. I hope no one sees me out here trying to get his attention. How embarrassing.* Arnetta bent over, cupping her hands around her eyes, and pressed against the window. It must've blocked out any daylight because Craig jumped a little and jerked his head towards her. He gave her an instant smile and rolled the window down with his left hand while turning the music down with his right. She could hear the music now, whereas before all she could hear was the thump-thump from the additional speakers he'd added that took up almost all the rear dashboard. Arnetta smiled. *He's playing my song.*

Arnetta hurried around the car while Craig reached over and opened her door from the inside. She slid into the seat and savored the last of the song's soulful beat without saying a word until it was over. Craig turned off the radio and then turned to look at Arnetta.

"What?"

"You like Phil Collins?"

"Yes, especially this song. I just bought the tape for my Walkman. Well, it's the soundtrack from Miami Vice. There's something about those drums."

"So, you like drums." It was a statement, not a question. Craig turned toward Arnetta to finish, "I do too. I have a set in the basement-slash-family-room-slash-put-it-in-that-room-when-nobody-knows-where-else-to-put-it room."

Arnetta laughed. *I really like this guy. I'm attracted to his cute face, sure, but I think I really enjoy being with him. He seems to get me; he doesn't back away when his buddies walk up while we're talking. He could be with practically any girl in school, yet here I am, sitting in his incredible car. Oh, I've seen him talking to other girls, but he doesn't stand as close to them as he does me.* Arnetta removed her glasses to try to get a smudge off using her shirttail. Craig reached over and put a finger under her chin, gently lifting her head up. She turned to face him. Their faces were so close, they had to look from eye to eye, but no closer. It was close enough for Arnetta to see without her glasses, and since she's very

153

near sighted, it was very close. Close enough to see the little brown flecks in his otherwise sea-blue eyes. *Well, he looks like he likes what he sees. I sure like what I see.*

"Ever thought about getting contacts?"

Spell broken. Broken into a million pieces. Arnetta sighed. Looking down, she noticed she'd made the smudges worse on her glasses. She had been so relaxed. As soon as his question reached her ears, her hand automatically tried to assume her balled-fist reaction, but since she was holding her glasses, they looked more like the talons of a bird of prey. She brought her glasses up to her mouth, breathing a mist of fog onto them, wiping them clean, and adjusting them on the bridge of her nose.

"Yes. I have. I just haven't had the extra money yet. And besides, I don't even know if I can wear contacts or not. I will probably try them one day, though."

As if Craig sensed he'd shattered a perfect moment, he straightened up in his seat. "I'm only asking because you have such beautiful eyes, Arnetta. It's a shame you have to hide them behind those glasses."

Should've quit while you were ahead, Craig. "Thanks." Arnetta mustered up a little smile that never reached her eyes.

Craig put one hand on the steering wheel and the other on the gearshift. "Where to, M'Lady?"

Oh, he's quick. Trying to lighten the mood. OK, I can play that game. "Main Street, Sir, and no dilly-dallying around." This time the smile lifted her eyes. She hoped he could see them behind those glasses.

He kept looking over at Arnetta while he was driving. When she'd return the glance, he'd look at the road again. *Him with that Sonny Crockett smile, his blonde hair a little shaggy around his collar. Man, does he ever look hot. Him. This car. Him IN this car....*

"So, Arnetta. What's the scoop with this Winter Dance everyone's so hyped up about? Is it any good?"

Arnetta held out her hand flat and waved it back and forth. "Eh, so-so, I guess. I went to one in the Ninth Grade, but I didn't go last year. They're OK, I guess." *In the Ninth grade, everybody goes as a class. It's sort of a rite of passage thing, so hardly anyone has a date. Tenth grade is different, a whole different story. If you don't have a date by the week before, you need to either start making it clear you have other plans or go by yourself and be prepared to be gawked at when you show up alone. There are a few of the super cool dudes that can pull off going alone and still be the life of the party, but it's not as easy when you're a girl. Besides, when a guy goes alone, he sort of gets a free ride. No flowers to buy, no dinner to buy, and no pressure to stick with one person for the whole night. Guys have it easy. If I was a guy...Uh Oh. Craig's talking. What did I miss while I was in deep with my inner pathetic self?* Arnetta smiled a little and nodded in response. *Think Arnetta. What's he asking? Was I planning to go on the senior trip to France? Did I like David Bowie's song, Let's Dance? Oh great. Blew it. Now I can't say 'Huh?' because I already nodded. Here I go, making a fool out of myself.* "What? I'm sorry, I was lost in the music, I guess. I wasn't paying attention. I mean, I was, but I got lost in the music, I guess."

Craig looked back and forth between her, the road, and then to the radio, which was still turned off. Arnetta could feel the heat in her face. *No, no, no, please don't blush.*

"Are you serious? You really didn't hear me?"

"I was deep in thought, Craig. I'm sorry."

She noticed his Adam's apple bob up and down, and he had a weird look on his face like he was up in front of the class about to recite Chaucer or something.

"Ground Control to Arnetta. Arnetta, are you in there?"

She smiled, appreciating his good nature. "You have my undivided attention Ground Control. Go ahead."

"What I said was, I think I'd like to go to the Winter Dance this year. Do you want to go?"

Arnetta could've sworn she heard fireworks, the church tower bells ringing, and a heavenly choir of angels singing the Hallelujah chorus all at the same time. *Did he just ask me to the Winter Dance?* Then replacing the celebration, she heard the train whistle, the brakes screeching to a halt, and a big red stop sign. *Not so fast, Arnetta. He said, do you want to go, not do you want to go with me.*

"Um, maybe. I hadn't really thought about it, Craig." Looking out the window, she noticed they were nearing Main Street. *Oh, this is bad. Really bad. Now, if he was asking me, I may have blown it. Why can't guys just say what they mean? No. You need to add two little words, Craig. "Do you want to go to the dance? It's not enough. Say it. Please say what I'm hoping you meant. Just two little words... "with me." Think. Think. Think.* She turned back to him, put on a coy smile, and fanned her face with her hand like a true southern belle, "It's just that I've had so many offers, I'd hate to have to pick just one." She burst out laughing at her own joke, hoping he'd join.

He wasn't laughing, but he didn't look mad either. "Well, I was hoping you wouldn't pick one...of those other offers, Arnetta. I was hoping you'd go with me."

Now THAT I heard loud and clear. Yes. Yes. Yes! Smiling, trying not to look overjoyed, but figured it wasn't working, and she didn't really care. A little pip escaped her throat. *How embarrassing.* Almost like a hiccup, it's the sound one makes when they're so excited, a word tries to rush out of the mouth before the brain tells it what to say.

"Excuse me!" covering her mouth, pretending it was a hiccup, "I had a Coke at lunch, must've drunk it too fast. Yes. Yes, Craig, I would love to go to the Winter Dance with you." Glancing out the car window to give her stomach a chance to quit doing somersaults, she noticed the What's New sign hanging over the sidewalk.

"Oh, STOP! Here we are. We're here, Craig. Sorry. This is where I'm going."

He looked in his rearview mirror and pulled over into a parking spot. "What in the heck happened here?" The concrete was busted up, a big crater where the parking meter had been, flanked by two orange cones.

"Oh, that? See, that's what I was telling you about. Brinda? My new friend? She was driving, and something happened, she jumped the curb and knocked over the parking meter."

"Wow, how fast was she going? She really did a number."

"She said her brakes gave way, and she turned in to avoid running into the back of someone."

"I'd say. Wow. That or your new friend was trying to fly. Is she here? Does she work here or something?"

That old green-eyed monster called jealousy tried to creep up Arnetta's back and tap her on the shoulder. She squashed it hard. *You're not welcome in my head, now go away!* "Yes, I'm meeting her here, but she doesn't work here. She's just meeting me here. You want to come in and meet her? I'd like you to meet my other friend too."

"Other friend?"

"Yeah, you remember me telling you about my friend, L.M. Mr. Little Mann?"

"Oh, yeah. The real little man. Oh, that's right, this is his place. Yeah, sure. Why not? I've got a few minutes to kill before I go home and change for work."

"Work? Did you get an after-school job? Arnetta was picturing him bagging groceries, delivering pizzas...

"Yeah, I cut grass for a few people. About ten people now, I guess. They keep me pretty busy, gets slower now though since its winter, but there's usually some people that keep me on, raking leaves, clearing the garden, and my favorite job, cleaning gutters."

"Really? You actually like cleaning gutters?"

"No. I hate that part." They both laughed.

"I did not know you did that, Craig. Sounds like hard work." *So, now I know how you always have that gorgeous tan. Walking behind a mower with no shirt on.*

"It is hard work, but decent money. Gas ain't cheap, you know. I filled up the other day, and it was $1.20 a gallon!" He patted the dashboard, "By the time I get gas for Bella here, and fill up my tanks for the mower, it was nearly $25.00! Highway robbery if you ask me, but like I said, it's decent money. One job gets me a tank of gas. I try to keep them on a pretty tight schedule, so I've got money coming in every month."

Arnetta opened her door and stepped out. "Sounds like you've got a plan. That's great. Is your car is named Bella? That's cute."

"Yeah. Bella means beautiful." He smiled and patted the dashboard again.

"You coming? You can just say hi and bye if you'd like." *Well, if Bella means beautiful, I've just named your smile.*

Craig climbed out of his car and walked Arnetta around the hole in the sidewalk. His hand was at the small of her back. *Oh, that's nice. It's like I matter to him. Here I go, walking into a store full of things. Things that are cast-offs, just waiting to be the object of someone's affection. I think I'll fit right in.*

17

The Power of The Mirror

The little bell that hung on the inside of the door jingled to announce their entrance. Craig stood at the entrance, much like Arnetta did the first time she came into What's New. It took a minute to get adjusted to the dim interior, but that wasn't all, it took time to adjust to the smell of old furniture and the number of things to see.

Arnetta tugged at his jacket sleeve, "Come on, they're probably in the back."

Craig followed her towards the rear of the store while glancing from side to side. "This is like walking into someone's house, and all their belongings are at the front door!"

"I know, isn't it great?" Arnetta couldn't tell if Craig's look said 'Yeah' or "You're kidding, right?" "We can look around later. If you want."

L.M.'s office was a square cubicle with three old desks lining all walls except the entry wall, and it wasn't much of a wall at all, as it was made of floor to ceiling antique French doors. The old glass was almost wavy in places, causing a distorted image when looking through the panes. There were two fixed doors on each side of the working double doors in the center. Each door was only two feet wide, so you almost had to open both at the same time, giving the person entering a feeling of making a grand entrance. L.M.'s office and the bathroom next to it were the only places in the store with bright fluorescent lighting. The whole store used the lamps for sale as the main lighting, and there were lots of them. He left a few on all night, but not always the same ones. He went around and turned out the others in the store at five o'clock every day. It was almost a ritual, and he had a particular route. Arnetta helped him one evening, and she noticed he'd performed his duty with such care, almost as if he was tucking them into bed each night.

Both L.M. and Brinda looked up as Craig and Arnetta got closer. Brinda's head had been deep in an old Look magazine, and L.M. was doing bookwork. Arnetta sucked in her breath in an audible gasp when she noticed the mirror face down on the desk next to where Brinda was sitting. It was the same mirror she'd held when she saw the accident, the lady on the back of the mirror still beckoning.

"What's the matter?" Craig whispered. He was standing so close; she felt the heat of his words through her hair.

"Noth...Nothing." She opened the doors wide into the room, "Hi guys, I want you to meet my frie...this is Craig. Craig, this is Brinda, that's Brinda with an 'i' Arnetta gave an upward, sweeping gesture with an arm towards Brinda,

"And this is L.M." as she used her other arm towards L.M. Her inner self almost saying Ta-Da!

L.M. scooted off his chair and waddled over to Craig with an extended hand, which Craig grasped as they both said, 'Nice to meet you.' *Well, I'm impressed. Craig definitely went to Manners School. I don't know what I expected, but I know some guys at school who would've turned this opportunity into an embarrassing situation, like trying to give a high-five instead of a handshake.*

Brinda sat back in her chair; she was eyeing Craig up-and-down like she was trying to figure out if he was worth the purchase. "C-r-aig?" She drew out his name in one lengthy question mark that could've easily said 'you old sly devil.' *Uh oh. Not good, Brinda, please don....* "Arnetta, you've been keeping secrets again." Arnetta felt the heat from her neck backwash to the tip of her head. "No, I haven't Brinda. I've told you about Craig." She looked over at Craig and gave a sheepish smile. *Oh great. Now he thinks I talk about him all the time. I think about him a lot, but I really don't talk about him that much. Do I?* Craig seemed to be enjoying the moment a little too much.

Brinda kept it up, pouring it on thick, "I know you *told* me about him, but you didn't say how cute he was." She stood up and faced Craig toe-to-toe. She kept her head lowered, so she had to look up at him through her thick black lashes.

Craig stepped back half an inch. Not quite far enough as Arnetta would've liked, but far enough to show Brinda he wasn't biting. Not today, anyway. L.M. seemed to know this game as well, and he came to their rescue. "Craig, would you like to look around the place?" He'd raised his short arm up and panned it around as if surveying his kingdom.

"Thank you, but no. Not today. I've really got to get going. I've got to get to work. I just brought Arnetta by and didn't want to drive off without meeting you and saying hello."

L.M. started to grill him, "Work? Where? Where do you work?"

"Oh, yards. I cut yards, that's all. Just something to help me keep up my car."

Brinda piped in. "Ooh, I've heard about that car. That's your Mustang, right? Can I take it for a spin?"

Craig turned to Brinda, "Um, no offense Brinda, but I don't think so. I've seen how *your* driving ends up." He glanced at Arnetta and L.M. for affirmation and caught their smiles.

"Ouch, none taken." Brinda sort of growled and plopped back down in the seat, picking up the mirror while removing its cloth cover. "Hey, Arnetta. Did you tell Craig about the mirror too?"

Craig turned to Arnetta with a big question mark all over his face. "Mirror?" He faced Brinda and said, "What mirror?"

Arnetta and L.M. gave Brinda a wide-eyed stare, and she received the message loud and clear, but continued, "What? Craig, we were just getting ready to test out this mirror. Seems it has special powers or something. Your friend here says she saw the wreck I had before it actually happened. Now, I don't know about all that mumbo jumbo, but I can tell you for a fact that when I DID have the accident, Arnetta was right here in this store staring at me, but she claims she was down the stree..."

"Brinda, stop. Please," Arnetta cut her off, "Craig just came in to meet y'all, not hear your mumbo jumbo."

Craig took a step towards Brinda and the mirror. "No, Arnetta. It's OK. I've got a few minutes. So, tell me, Brinda. What kind of special powers are you talking about?"

Arnetta glanced at L.M. and then to her shoes. Her fisted hands by her side, she wished she could disappear. *Oh no! Brinda, what have you done? It's too soon. Craig will probably think I'm crazy after this. So much for his invitation to the dance, that's got more history in it than my history book.*

Undeterred. Brinda handed the antique piece, mirror-side down, to Craig. "Here, take a look. Tell me what you see."

Craig took the mirror, flipping it once, and with a skeptical look on his face, stared into the mirror. A huge smile came across his face, then he handed it back to Brinda the same way he received it, with the raised artwork on top.

"Well? What did you see?" Brinda asked, standing and closing the gap between her and Craig even closer than before.

"What did I see?" Craig, again took a step back while glimpsing at Arnetta, "I saw Arnetta at the winter dance, dancing with me."

Arnetta lifted her head as if Craig was her puppeteer and had jerked her head string. *What?*

Brinda took a step back as if she was retreating from battle, but not ready to surrender to the war. L.M. smiled, which seemed to fuel Brinda's retort, "Is that all? That's not so earth-shattering. Maybe you ought to look again, you know, give it a little time."

"No, Brinda, but thanks just the same. I really do have to go. Nice meeting you both." And then he turned to Arnetta, "See you tomorrow?"

"Yeah, sure, bye." Arnetta's eyes were fixed on Craig's back as he walked towards the door. Her gallant knight stepped into his red horse and drove away.

"DANG girl, you must be in love." Then Brinda continued to tease in a loud whisper, "Craig and Netta sitting in a tree, K-I-S-S-I-N-G, first comes love, then comes marriage, here comes Craig with a baby carriage."

L.M spoke up, "Arnetta, Craig seems like a fine young man, at first glance anyway. And it seems as if he's quite taken with you." When he'd said, 'taken with you,' he was talking to Arnetta, but turned and looked at Brinda. Arnetta smiled.

OK. That's a little too much attention on Craig and me, but I'd have to agree, he is fine. "L.M., Thanks. He's nice." *and he's nice to me too.* "Not to change the subject, but what's that mirror doing in here? Have y'all been..."

Brinda answered before L.M. had the chance. "No, Arnetta. We were waiting for you. I'm not going to lie, I wanted to, and I actually tried, but L.M. caught me and said we had to wait on you."

Arnetta turned towards L.M. with a grateful smile. *It's not my mirror, but I wonder if L.M. feels like I do in that the power of the mirror is between me and the mirror. I'm drawn to it.* "What do you mean you tried?

"L.M. said he wants to show me, but you have to be here too. He says I haven't found my muse yet."

"Your muse?"

"Arnetta," L.M. started, "You've probably read about them in Greek mythology. I just told Brinda that this mirror might be your muse of sorts. Brinda's muse hasn't appeared yet. A muse doesn't have to be an object; hers may appear as something else. It's always fascinating when you find your muse, but you can't sit around and wait for her to come to you. You have to go out and find her."

"Oh, so you're saying I sought out my own muse? I thought it was just a chance encounter, I mean I would never..." Arnetta patted L.M.'s hand and continued, "Sorry, L.M., but it's true. I would never have come into this store if that rainstorm hadn't happened so fast, and I hadn't left my raincoat at the dentist's office."

L.M. smiled as he reared back in his office chair. He'd laced his fingers behind his head, and he didn't say a word, but his smile spoke volumes.

Brinda butted in, "Wait a minute, L.M. You're saying it wasn't by chance? Cuz if you are, you're also saying my accident was not an accident after all. I can guarantee you I didn't wreck on purpose!"

L.M. sat up straight again. "I'm not saying anything. I just want you two to think about it. While you're thinking about it, let me tell you about another place and a different time."

Brinda and Arnetta looked at each other at the same time, gave a 'why not' shrug, signaling L.M. to go ahead with his story. Brinda spoke for both, "We'll bite, L.M., go ahead with your fairy tale."

"This is not a fairy tale, girls, it's also something I've never told anyone, except for one person and for two essential reasons. For one thing, no one would believe me, and the second reason is no would believe me, AND they'd most likely put me away. Why, if this had happened three hundred years ago, I'd be burned alive for what I'm about to say."

Arnetta pulled up a third chair, ready to hear his tale. Brinda, on the other hand was a little more skeptical.

"Oh, come on, guys. You gotta be kidding. Three hundred years ago? This *is* a fairy tale."

"I didn't say what I'm about to tell you happened three hundred years ago, Brinda. I said IF this story were told three hundred years ago, you'd be burned alive. What I'm about to tell you happened only five years ago."

Brinda pretended to have no interest by plastering a smirk on her face, but at the same time, she leaned in close to hear what L.M. had to say.

"I hadn't always been in the resale and antiques business, you know. I wandered in, much like you did Arnetta. I had no reason; it wasn't even raining. I was just drawn for some reason that day to come into the store. It wasn't called What's New back then, it was Bledsoe's Furniture Barn. Mrs. Bledsoe was a statuesque lady with white hair. She seemed like a matriarchal Amazon lady to me, very intimidating at first," Brinda and Arnetta exchanged a quick grin and eye roll as he continued, "After a quick look around, I spotted the mirror. That mirror. I reached for it, but old Mrs. Bledsoe grasped it as if she needed to examine the back of it. I forget now exactly what story she told me. I stayed a little while longer, then left and went home. That night I couldn't sleep. There was something odd about Mrs. Bledsoe, I knew it, but I couldn't put my finger on it. The next day, I returned to the store, we chatted a little more and then I found my chance. The phone rang, and Mrs. Bledsoe came right back here to answer. Being very casual, I meandered over towards the mirror, picked it up, and looked at it. What I saw was horrid! It was only a flash, you know, it happens almost faster than you can blink, and then it's gone. Just my own ugly mug was staring back at me." L.M. seemed to sink and lowered his head. "I saw..." he looked up with a frightened look on his face as if he'd just seen something terrifying. "I saw Governor Reagan get shot. It's like I was there. In one instant, I was hearing a shot so close to my head, I thought it was me, the next second, the mirror was a normal mirror again. I ran out the door and got home as soon as I could. The vision was so real. I'm not sure if I was there as a spectator, or if I was the shooter."

"Whoa! L.M., are you saying you think you shot President Reagan? Not possible. You were here, right?"

"Brinda, the day I saw him in the mirror, he was still Governor Reagan. He had just beat out Jimmy Carter and would be the next president of the United States. Yes. I was here in this very same place, the day I saw him in the mirror, the day I saw the vision. But here's the funny part. Well, nothing about it was funny, but strange. I had heard of premonitions before, but I'd never had any inkling of having any before. At that time, mind you, I still hadn't connected the mirror to the vision. Remember, the mirror was just a mirror, and the vision was only a second, a flash, at the time, it felt like a slow-motion playback, a mind-trick. I went home that day and turned on the TV. I was thinking maybe there'd be a special news bulletin or something, but there wasn't. I flipped the channels back and forth, but nothing about Mr. Reagan except the normal election mumbo jumbo. I thought about going to the police, but what could I have told them? The men in white coats would've been at my door in no time. I had many sleepless nights, let me tell you. I started following the news more carefully, paying attention to his schedule and stuff like that. I'd ask people everywhere I went if they knew where he'd be speaking next. On the one hand, I didn't want to be anywhere near him, but on the other hand, I was afraid if anything *did* happen, I may appear to have been stalking him. I didn't know what to do. Finally, after months of nothing, I chalked it up to a very vivid imagination." L.M. relaxed a little and let out a long sigh.

Brinda and Arnetta were rapt in the story. "And?" Arnetta asked, "Is there more?"

"Yes. The next year, just a couple of months after Reagan was sworn in as our 40th president, it happened, just like in my vision. I'll never forget that day. March 30, 1981. He was just outside of the Washington Hilton, and of course, surrounded by secret service and others. The shooter was there, but thankfully, it wasn't me that pulled the trigger. When I think back to how close I came to going to the authorities, describing the gun, the day...everything in my vision came true. All I saw was Reagan go down as the secret service dove on top of him to keep him safe. I didn't know until after it happened that he would come out of that day alive. I felt responsible. That's the curse of the mirror. You see it happen, but you don't know *when* it will happen. The day of Reagan's assassination attempt, I don't mind telling you two, I went home and cried and vomited. The way the media blows everything out of proportion, I've always felt that if I had gone to the authorities, I might have somehow been linked and blamed for what happened that day. I'd most probably be behind bars."

Arnetta's face was white as a sheet. She looked at Brinda. *The bruising is all but gone, but I still remember the feeling of watching the terror on Brinda's face as the wreck was happening. The wreck I saw before it happened.*

L.M. continued, "Mrs. Bledsoe knew somehow, I could feel it. I don't know how she knew or when she knew, but she knew. Old Mrs. Bledsoe got me to tell her the story, and she's been the only one, until today. After the assassination attempt, she sat me down and told me there was a proper way to use the mirror. I remember thinking, 'now you tell me.' I only saw visions a few more times, and none were as dramatic as the first time. I ended up buying the place from Mrs. Bledsoe. She wanted to spend her remaining years out in Phoenix near her family. We exchanged Christmas cards a couple of years, but in the third year, my card was returned with `no longer at this address, no forwarding address known` stamped on it. Sometimes, people just appear in your life, stay for a little while, and then leave. You two should get used to that, it's called life."

Arnetta wanted to add, *Oh, I know all about people staying in your life for a little while and then leaving*, but something else piqued her attention. "L.M., what did she mean about the *proper way* to use the mirror?"

"Well, I'm not sure about all this, but she told me it had something to do with the way you pick it up, not just the speed, but the angle in which it's held. You may not have noticed, but when you picked up the mirror, I sort of backed away. I didn't want you to see me in the mirror, and if I'd been closer, the angle could've caught me in the reflection too." He looked over towards Brinda, "Sorry, Brinda, I had no idea what she would see, or even what she *did* see. Only one person can see."

173

Arnetta couldn't seem to make rhyme or reason of what he'd just said. "So, wait a minute. Are you saying if you were in the image I saw, I might have seen something happening to you in the future?

You wouldn't want to know your future?"

"Without a doubt, I can tell you that I have no interest in finding out what will happen in the indeterminable future. None whatsoever. It could drive you crazy, girls. It makes people do strange and dangerous things. For instance, Mrs. Bledsoe told me later of someone she knew that once had the mirror, it practically destroyed a whole family. Greed, power, alcoholism, drug addiction, and other dangerous behaviors, it all happens. Think about it, girls, if you saw something in your future, would you be as careful with the present? Or if you saw something terrible happen to you or someone you love; how would you live with the fear of the unknown circumstances that led to that point? Many people live daily with fear of the unknown, and that's bad enough in itself, pure torture for some people. But, if you *know* what's going to happen, just not when? That's a whole other ball of wax. The mirror is dangerous and should not be taken lightly. If you want to try to see some things, I know some tricks I can share with you.

Arnetta looked at Brinda and found her staring back at her, searching her face as well. It was as if they were sending each other telepathic messages. *Do we want to know how to use this mirror? I feel like this is a precious gift somehow, but what if...what if? Does Brinda have the same expectations, or would she be in it for the thrill?* Her concentration was interrupted by L.M.

"Are you ready?"

As if this were part of some kind of solemn ceremonial oath, both girls turned their gaze to L.M. and said in unison, "We're ready."

For the next hour and a half, L.M. showed them how hand movements control the timing of the mirror's reflection, but he started off by again, telling them the seriousness of the mirror. He also said to them that not everyone has the gift of sight. "I believe we three were brought together for a reason. I don't believe in coincidence at all, everything happens for a reason, and every person we meet is for a purpose, whether it's a minute in passing or a lifetime of interaction. It's your responsibility to keep this to yourselves. As I said, some people would try to use this for their own fame and fortune, and I don't think its purpose was meant for that. Another crucial element, remember, I said that not everyone has the gift of sight? Well, even *your* sight can come and go, it doesn't work like a coin-operated device, it cannot be forced."

The mirror was covered with a brown felt cloth the whole time L.M. demonstrated the process. "You always return the mirror face down. If you want to use it simply as a mirror, it's picked up slowly and with one fluid motion. A quick flip to the right and you may get a vision of something happening in the next week."

"That's what I did. I guess. Right, L.M.?"

"That's exactly what you did, Arnetta. Of course, I didn't know until after you saw something that you *could* see something. That's the exact moment I knew we were destined to meet each other. Now let's carry on. If you flip the mirror twice to the right, like this," and he made a motion like someone would use the hand signal for *maybe so, maybe not,* "you know like you were trying to decide if you wanted to look in the mirror and got distracted, then decided to go ahead. Anyway, two flips and you will see something that will happen in the next month or so. Now here's the tricky part..."

Brinda interjected, "As if that's not tricky enough?"

L.M. smiled, "It will all come in time. If you pick it up and flip it quickly to the left, you may see something that will happen within the next year, and two quick flips may reveal an event within two to ten years."

"How are we ever going to learn this?" Arnetta was flipping her bare hand this way and that way, "And how would you ever decide in the first place which way to flip it? It's only a second or two" she turned to Brinda, "But I can tell you those two seconds were in slow motion when I saw you wreck! It seemed like it was several minutes!"

"That's just it, girls." L.M. placed the mirror back on the desk, "After the novelty wears off, you may not want to see anything at all. It can drive you crazy. Just because you can see the future, it's only a snippet, you don't know what led up to that point, or what happens after, and you can't change any of it. Possession of this mirror doesn't make you a superhero."

Arnetta sat up straight and cocked her head as if on alert. She heard something. She stood up and walked to the office door. She turned back to L.M. and Brinda, "Brinda, that's the grandfather clock I heard going off. It's five o'clock, we better get going. By the time we get home, it'll be time for dinner, and you haven't been properly introduced to Gummy and Papaw yet."

Brinda made no move to get up, but she turned towards L.M. and kept her eyes on him while she spoke to Arnetta, "L.M. said I could stay here at the store for a while."

Arnetta's eyes ping-ponged between the two, "But why? Why would you want to stay here? In a store? That's crazy. Is it the sleeping arrangement at my house? We can do better than just a pallet on the floor if you want. I guess we could both sleep in my bed." *Now I feel bad I didn't think of that last night.*

L.M. came to Brinda's aide, "Arnetta, I told her she could stay here. There's a little room back behind here with a kitchenette, it's adjacent to the bathroom. Brinda pulled a

177

chaise lounge from the showroom in there. It's not much, but it's fine for a few days." He turned to Brinda, "But remember, like I said, after I go home, this old place has night noises like you wouldn't believe. I swear this old furniture talks to one another when I'm gone. I used to stay late sometimes and do bookwork, there are more creaks in this joint than in my leg on a cold winter morning."

"I'll be fine, L.M., believe me after you've slept in your car, or in the woods, you get used to noises and things that go bump in the night."

"Arnetta, tell you what," L.M. walked towards Arnetta, "I will be leaving here in a few minutes anyway. Why don't I take you home, or at least until you're almost home? That way, we can have a few more minutes to put the mirror to the test, maybe you will see something good this time. I'd like for you to see that it's not always a bad vision. What do you say?"

"Sure. OK, I can do that." Arnetta looked at Brinda, trying to read her mind. *This place is a little creepy during the day, why would anyone want to stay here all night?*

18

Visions

L.M., Brinda, and Arnetta walked out into the show-room. To make sure they weren't disturbed, L.M. walked to the front door and flipped the sign from OPEN to CLOSED. Each of them found a comfortable chair and settled in as if they were preparing to watch a show. L.M. placed the mirror face-down on top of a vanity nearby.

"OK, so who's going to go first?" Brinda asked, trance-like, not taking her eyes off the mirror.

"Man, you've got it bad, don't you? You just can't wait to see what you can see, can you? I bet you're the first in line at the Halloween carnival's crystal ball booth, too, huh?" *Maybe that was a little harsh. I don't know why this irks me so much, but it does.*

L.M. must have sensed a little tension and offered, "Brinda, yes, why don't you go first. This is your first time, and who knows? You may not even have the sight."

Brinda smiled at Arnetta with her best get-over-it smile, and then turned towards L.M. and answered with the most insincere sincerity, "No, L.M. I think you or Arnetta should go first so I can watch. I'd hate to mess something up."

"Oh, you can't hurt anyth..."

"Oh, for goodness sakes! I'll go!" *Geez, L.M. doesn't understand at all. He has no idea when he's being played.* "Sorry, L.M. I-I don't know what came over me." She was talking to L.M. but staring daggers into Brinda. *Am I jealous? And if I am, of what? Craig? L.M.? The mirror? What is it about Brinda that drives me crazy?*

Brinda hands crept up, her fingers wriggling and in a slow deep voice, said, "It's the power of the mirror." Brinda couldn't keep a straight face, and soon, all three were laughing.

L.M. broke the mood. "Girls, I understand your curiosity, I do. I've been in the same shoes as both of you. Brinda, I, myself, was itching to turn to the mirror after I realized the potential, and Arnetta, even after I saw what I saw that was so troubling, I found myself going back time after time. I didn't always understand what the mirror wanted to show me. Sometimes, I longed to see something, anything, just for the thrill, and it seemed like it was those times, all I saw was myself. Just like any other mirror."

Arnetta walked over to the desk where the mirror lay. She picked it up with her right hand, just as she'd done before, except this time, she didn't turn it over to look into it. Remembering the horrific image she'd seen the first time, she laid the mirror back down. She took a deep breath, her hand still grasping the handle. She traced the carved image of the girl on the backside of the mirror with her left hand. *So beautiful. What do you want with me?*

"Arnetta, are you OK?" Brinda seemed genuinely concerned, as she stood and took a step towards Arnetta

Arnetta nodded without taking her eyes off the mirror, memories flashed through her mind. *What am I waiting for?* She could feel the hairs on her neck pinging. She dropped her left arm by her side to hopefully conceal her balled fist. *This is stupid. This is like that time we had that Ouija board, and I got freaked out because I was sure the planchette was really speaking to me from the dead. Man, I haven't thought about that night for a long time.*

Seventh grade. I'd been invited to a spend-the-night party at Sally Rivers' house. I was so excited they'd asked me. We had all piled into Dunfergott's Pizza and Movies video store and ended up with a Risky Business video starring Tom Cruise, Blue Lagoon with Brooke Shields, and E.T. with Drew Barrymore and that cute little alien. We knew then, it was way too many movies because some of the other girls were bringing games also. Sally's mom ordered pizzas, and when we got home, we discovered she'd made double fudge brownies. It was like a heaven of indulgence. We'd all changed into our pajamas and claimed our spot with sleeping bags, palettes, or beds. There were tons of

Pepsi and Mountain Dew, popcorn, Nerds, and Nachos to keep us going for days. It was my first sleepover, and I only knew one of the girls, Elaine.

We never even finished one whole movie. We'd start one, and one of the group would complain it was stupid, or slow, or something. Disregarding the Be Kind and Rewind sticker on the VHS tape, we just moved on to another one, you could tell Sally was used to handling the remote control.

With pizza boxes opened and spread all over the floor, videotapes left out of their boxes, paper plates, plastic cups with our names written on them, and other snack stuff all over the floor, one of the girls, Missy, I think announced it was time for games. Sally pulled out her Ouija board. Everyone had played before except me. Everyone took turns asking questions like, will my parents get a divorce, does so-and-so like me, and then it got serious. Someone had the bright idea to talk to the dead. Since no one else in the room had family members that had died, except for old grandparents, they had chosen Arnetta to be the one to talk to the dead through the Ouija board. Everyone was to come up with a question. I had been as caught up in it like everyone else.

Sally and I sat across the board from each other, each with our fingertips on the planchette. Sally asked the question of the board, "Why did Arnetta's family all die at the same time?" I remember my fingers hopping off the planchette as if they'd been dunked in boiling water. And I remember Sally's response. "Don't move your fingers, Arnetta. You'll spoil the answer." I did what I was told, against my better judgment. Sally asked the same question, "Why did Arnetta's family all die at the same time?" All the other girls hung over the Ouija board in anticipation. My veins were filled with dread. The game piece started to move as it spelled out the answer.

Y-O-U S-H-O-U-L-D H-A-V-E B-E-E-N W-I-T-H U-S

The party was over for Arnetta. Retreating to the living room sofa of an unknown house, filled with people she barely knew, wrapping her arms around her knees, pulling them as close to her body as possible to shield her. Shield her from what? The girls in the other room, or the dreaded answer? The answer she'd known all along as the truth. Arnetta had always wondered why she had been spared when her whole family vanished in one day.

Arnetta found out later that year that the whole Ouija board thing had been a hoax. *I remember that conversation like it was yesterday.* "Arnetta, I've got to tell you something." It was Elaine. She had caught up with me as I was hurrying out of school.

"What's up?"

"I don't want you to be mad."

"Ok. Well, I can't be mad or not be mad unless you tell me."

"It's just that..."

"Elaine, what is it? It can't be that bad, can it? I mean on a scale of one-to-ten, how mad could I be?"

"I don't know, but I've just got to tell you. Ever since... well, ever since Sally River's spend-the-night party, well, you just haven't been the same. It's like you're living on another planet."

"Yeah, so? Is that it? You trying to be my guidance counselor? Mrs. Hall wouldn't like you stepping into her territory." I laughed it off, "OK, well, to make you feel better. That's like a one on the scale. I better get going, see ya."

"Arnetta, wait!" Elaine reached out and tapped my shoulder. "That's not it. I mean, that's not all."

She had my attention then. "What's not all?"

Elaine looked me straight in the eyes and said, "Sally and everybody else got me to ask you over for the sleepover. They said it would be fun. The Ouija board was their idea, and they said you'd get a kick out of it, and afterward we'd all laugh about it, and that you'd know it was fake, I mean, who wouldn't? After you ran off in the other room and barely spoke the rest of the time, we all decided not telling you it was fake would be better. The plan was to tell you later, but it kept dragging on and on, and I'm worried about you because you haven't seemed like your old self since then. Arnetta, I'm sorry. I feel horrible."

Yeah, I got a kick out it all right. That night kicked my butt. Now, here I am, standing in front of this mirror with the same uneasiness I felt using that Ouija board. This time I'm hoping. Hoping for tomorrow and the day after, and the day after that. Hope is what I'd lost when my family left me, for all practical purposes, alone.

Arnetta steadied herself, took another deep breath, and picked up the mirror with a quick flip to the right and looked into the foreboding looking glass. After a second, a full, ear-raising smile covered her face. She could hear Brinda in the background talking, but her voice was muffled as if she were in the next room. *No, it's me. I'm in another place. I'm standing in a store with clothes on racks.* Arnetta moved her head around. This is a fancy store! There's a large raised oval pedestal with a mannequin and a long Cheval mirror at the end of another larger raised platform. The floor model is wearing the most beautiful purple dress I've ever seen. Stepping up, walking closer to the mannequin, I can see myself wearing this deep purple gown. It's a knee-length satin dress with puffed sleeves that end at my elbow with a silver tie. A matching silver tie is woven through the material and rests just below my boobs. I've never worn a neckline like this before, wow! Arnetta placed her palm on her bare upper chest. It's like something from the movies, from the empire waist, it's like the smooth material floats up to my shoulders. *All this skin needs a necklace, and I think I've got the perfect one.* Now, I'm seeing myself wearing this same dress dancing with Craig. He looks unbelievably handsome, and he keeps looking at me like...

"Arnetta, what do you see, what is it?"

The vision seemed to float away as she heard Brinda. Loud and clear. Placing the mirror back on the vanity, she turns and looks at L.M. and Brinda. *I feel like I just woke up from a dream, half in, half out of it still.* After a moment and a quick shake of her head, she was back.

"I just saw the most beautiful dress, y'all. It's got to be the dress I'm going to wear to the dance."

"Dance? What dance?"

Arnetta sat down and told them both that Craig had invited her to be his date at the school's Winter Dance. *Wait a minute. The Arnetta in the vision, wearing that dress, had a huge smile on her face. It was a radiant look. I can still sort of feel it. No, more than just a radiant look, it was an over-the-top-all-over-happy-look. I felt accepted. I felt loved.*

Now, it was Brinda's turn. She picked it up with her left hand and flipped it over as if to look into it, then turned it over and back again. Two flips.

Arnetta and L.M. volleyed looks between themselves and Brinda. After a silence that lasted an eternity of maybe sixty seconds, L.M. spoke first, "Well, Brinda? Did you see anything? Was it that bad or was it that good? You look like someone just licked the red off your candy."

Brinda glanced up through her lashes, and a tiny smirk was forming on one corner of her mouth. "Well, I guess you could say a little of both, L.M. The best part for me was the feeling I had when I was inside the mirror, at least that's what it felt like to me. It was like I was floating on a cloud; more vivid than any dream I've ever had. It's like I was between something good and better. I don't know how else I can explain it, it was just plain wonderful. I saw my mom, and she was the happiest I'd ever seen her, but the weird part is, she was playing Bingo inside the Qualla Boundary's Recreation Center, and we don't play Bingo for money there- it's not allowed."

"Well?" Arnetta asked, "Are you going to tell us more?"

Brinda sat up and recounted her vision.

"Well, here goes nothing. I saw a lady. A lady in a huge room filled with people. Then I thought, *wait. It's my mother! I almost didn't recognize her, she's so beautiful!* The last few years haven't been kind to my mother. She'd stopped taking care of herself, seemed depressed and walked around with a furrowed brown, slumped over, and a constant scowl on her face. Sometimes, she went days without bathing, and some days hardly got out of bed. *How can a person be so sad and angry all the time? Of course, I blame*

Dad, nothing is ever good enough for him. I think Mama just gave up. I've always been told Cherokee women rank better than most women when it comes to equality, but my dad doesn't care much for tradition anymore. In the mirror, I kept thinking, Mama, look at you now! I mean, there's my mom standing up in front of all these people, smiling the brightest smile I've ever seen. Her clothes look fresh, her makeup was perfect, and her shoulder-length black hair was full of shine and bounce. When I finally focused on the image on the wall behind my mother, I couldn't believe what I was really seeing. Bingo! My mother was holding up two fistfuls of cash. *'Mama, you're a winner!' Wait. That's strange. I know that building, but they don't have Bingo, not the kind that pays out money anyway.* And that's when the vision faded away. I was thinking, no, don't go, I want to see more. Sometimes, I feel like a small boat on a calm river, a boat filled with stones, destined to sink. Even though the vision itself was happy, so happy, as soon as it started to fade, I could feel my heart sink. Like when the final descent of the boat on that calm river sounded a thud, reverberating on the silent river bottom. No one to hear it but me. I felt my mother's sadness in the present time, then I realized the person in the boat was my mother. I wanted to jump back in the vision and yell, 'Mama, you were gambling, you're a winner, and you like it, and you're so happy! A happiness that doesn't come from one experience, you're glowing like this isn't the first day you are this happy. This is a glow that comes from a life transformation.' But then, I realized I can't go back to that vision, only revisit it in my mind. What happens to her between now and then? How long will I have to wait until I can see this glimpse of the future become a reality?" Brinda walked over and returned the mirror face down on the vanity. "I know what I'll do. It's what I have to do. I'll call my mom and let her know everything will be OK. I'll have to be careful how I tell her though, I can't just call her up out of the blue and say, 'Hey Mama. I saw the future today, and you know what? You're going win big, don't worry about a thing.' Nope. That wouldn't work. Mama's smart. She always used to tell me she could read me easier than the newspaper, so I'll need to choose my words carefully." Brinda shuffled her feet, looked around, and then plopped herself down in the overstuffed armchair, and crossed her arms. "When I looked into the mirror, I felt so calm, so at peace. The mirror seemed somehow to transport me to the place I was seeing, I felt it in all my senses, and what a wonderful feeling it was. But now I'm back to reality, back to normal, and it stinks big time."

L.M. reminded her, "Lest you forget, Brinda, things can change in an instant, but sometimes things take a little longer. I noticed you flipped the mirror to the left twice."

"That's right, so now I've got to wait two years for this, this vision, or whatever it is to come true? That's a crappy rule if you ask me."

"Not necessarily, Brinda. Yes, you've got to wait two years, but maybe even up to ten years. I didn't make up the rules if that's what you want to call them."

"Well, it stinks if you ask me. My mom shouldn't have to wait to be as happy as I saw her, she deserves all that and more, now!"

Arnetta broke the tension, "L.M., aren't you going to look in the mirror? C'mon, it's your turn."

L.M. slid out of his chair and waddled over to the vanity. He put his hands in his pockets and stood there for half a minute and then turned to the girls. "Every time I look in this mirror, I swear it's for the last time. I've seen some beautiful things, but I've also seen the terrible ones too. There's not a thing in this world you can do to change anything you see you know, at least I don't perceive how you could. There's something out of this world going on with this mirror, be it supernatural or divine intervention, I don't know, but I *do* know that it's way beyond the realm of my understanding. The fact is, no one understands. I genuinely believe it's up to us to keep the mirror as secret as possible, and I've always felt that way. The mirror chooses us to some degree, we don't get to choose the mirror. There's some reason it chose us, the three of us, and we need to keep it to ourselves. If word gets out, the mirror could fall into the wrong hands. Who's to say someone with ulterior motives won't get hold of the mirror and try to use it illegally? We can't let that happen. The best way for that not to happen is to keep the mirror between us.

"OK, OK, L.M., we get the picture, OK? We swear. Are you going to make us pinky swear too?" Brinda held up her pinky to show her sincerity.

L.M. dropped his head forward a notch and peered over the top of his wire-framed glasses, "No Brinda, but I'm serious. This has got to be an agreement between us three." He looked from Brinda to Arnetta and back. "Deal?"

"Yes, I agree," Arnetta replied.

In a more somber tone, Brinda countered, "Yes. Me too."

L.M. turned toward the vanity and started to pick up the mirror, but twisted around to face the girls when he overheard Arnetta murmur to Brinda, "I think we should come up with a word to remind us, you know, just in case we forget." Brinda rolled her eyes, and sighed a laugh, "You mean like a secret code word, Arnetta? Are you serious? Are we going to have a secret handshake too?"

"Stop, it's not funny. I was just thinking a word, or maybe a phrase...OK, picture this: Say one day, you and me are at the movies. A scene comes on that reminds one of us about something we've seen in the mirror, so we say, *Hey, that's just like you said you saw in the mirror.* Then the other one would say something like..." Arnetta searched the air for inspiration, "something like *red birds don't sing at night,* I don't know, I can't think of anything right now, but that's what I mean."

L.M. saved the day. "Girls, how about an acronym? When I was following the Reagan shooting, I came across the term POTUS. Do you know what that means? Both girls looked at each other and shrugged, signifying their answer, so he continued. "POTUS is another way for the secret service agents to refer to the President of the United States. POTUS was first used in telegraph messages in the late 1870s, and here we are in 1985, and most people have never heard of it. A word or phrase isn't bad, Arnetta, but an acronym is a whole sentence in a word, so to speak, so let's think about that, shall we?"

They brainstormed for a few minutes, and then Arnetta bubbled over with, "I've got one! How about misty? Like M-I-S-T-Y?

"Misty?" questioned L.M. and Brinda in unison.

"Yeah. Mirror Is Special. Thank You."

"Well, isn't that polite." Brinda deadpanned.

"OK, well, you come up with one better."

Again, L.M. mediated their conversation. "I kind of like M-O-D. You know, like Mirror-of-Destiny. But we don't have to come up with anything this afternoon, girls. Just think about it. Now, if I can have a minute, I think I'll take a look in this mirror. Just one more time. You both saw good things, so while we're on a roll..." He picked up the mirror, and like Brinda, he flipped it to the left, but only once before looking into it.

A quick smile came across his face, but that changed just as fast as it had appeared. It was as if he was being hypnotized because while holding onto the mirror, it appeared L.M. was trying to turn his face away, even though his head would turn, his eyes were fixed on whatever he was seeing. It was horrible, it was apparent by the terror in his eyes his vision was awful! He shook his head slowly back and forth. His left hand held the mirror in a white-knuckled grip while his right hand went to cover his gaping mouth, then that hand dropped to cover his chest. Before Arnetta or Brinda had a chance to say anything, L.M. crumpled to the floor, the mirror landing safely on top of him still clutched in his hand.

Arnetta screamed as she rushed to his side, "L.M., L.M.! What's wrong? Brinda?"

Brinda joined her and then took the mirror from his hand and replaced it on the vanity when she did, she must've noticed L.M.'s coloring. "Arnetta, his face is awfully white, even his lips are pale. Quick! Call 9-1-1! Call 9-1-1!"

Arnetta was already on her way to the office to call for help when she heard Brinda's words, "I think he's dying! Hurry!" The few seconds it took to reach the phone seemed to go in slow motion to Arnetta.

"9-1-1, what's your emergency?"

"Yes, my friend, L.M. He fell, I think he's dying. I don't know what to do, please hurry!"

"Miss, miss, calm down. What is your address?"

"I don't know, I don't know...." Turning to Brinda, "What's the address here, do you know?" then back in the phone receiver, "I know it's on Collier Street, just off Main Street. It's a store. It's called What's New. Please hurry."

"Miss, we know where that is, help is on the way."

While Arnetta was on the phone, Brinda ran to the front door and unlocked it, opened it up wide, and propped it open with a brass umbrella stand. Arnetta could see her run out onto the sidewalk and look up and down the street as if they'd be there the instant they were called.

The 9-1-1 dispatch lady asked Arnetta if L.M. was breathing. "He was. I don't know. He just dropped to the floor, is someone coming?"

"Yes, they are on the way now. Is there someone that can go outside to help the paramedics find the right place?"

"Someone is already out there looking for them. Hold on." Arnetta slammed the phone receiver on the desk and ran over to L.M. "L.M., just hold on. Don't you dare die on me! Help is on the way, OK? You're going to be all right." She thought she saw him blink, but it may have been her blinking to keep a tear from escaping the terror in her own eyes. She jumped up and raced to the phone, "He's still not moving, but I think I saw him blink, please hurry, his face is...please hurry!"

Her reply came when she heard the distinct wailing of the Landreth ambulance siren as it sped up the street. Brinda probably could've helped land a plane the way she was jumping up and down and waving her arms.

A paramedic ran in first to check L.M. out as two other men in blue rushed in the door right behind him with a gurney. They had L.M. strapped on in less than two minutes with an oxygen mask over his nose and mouth. They whizzed by her and carried him out the door. L.M.'s keys had fallen out of his pocket and were dangling from the gurney's edge. He wasn't moving at all. Arnetta grabbed the keys and looked at the dying man in passing. *L.M., please don't die. Don't you leave me too.* The sirens started again as the ambulance left. Arnetta jumped as she heard all the clocks in the store sound the hour. Six o'clock. She scanned the store for Brinda, who had made herself scarce earlier, leaving Arnetta to give the paramedic as much information as she could. She realized just about the only pertinent data she knew was his name. She didn't know any next of kin, insurance information, and certainly not his blood type. *I know they were just doing their job, but they sure made me feel inept. Next time I meet someone new, I'll be sure to ask all those questions first. Gummy always says, "A friend in need is a friend indeed." L.M. is my friend, and he needs me, but I feel like I let him down by not knowing more about him. Hang on, L.M.*

Arnetta and Brinda closed up the store. They decided it would be better to not go to the hospital just yet. "Brinda, remember how long it took you in the emergency room? Well, you probably don't because you were pretty much out of it, but it was a long time, but I bet it's going to be a long time for L.M. too. What should we do? I need to go home, or I'll have a lot of explaining to do. I gave them my phone number and told them to call me in case of an emergency."

Brinda gave a little humph before she answered, "Emergency? I hope there aren't any more emergencies. We'll just go see him in the morning then, OK? I'll stay here, like L.M. and I planned."

"OK. Probably not in the morning though, school, remember?"

"You can ditch school, Arnetta, who would know?"

"Um. Me, my teachers, Gum..."

"OK, OK. After school then. I'll just meet you at the hospital right after school. Deal?"

"Deal."

At least that was the plan.

19

Time Heals All Wounds

Arnetta tried to sleep, but every time she closed her eyes, she'd see L.M. fall to the floor. She was scared to death he wasn't going to make it through the night. The very thought of being *scared to death* now held a new meaning for her. *I should be with him,* she'd thought off and on during the night, and one time went as far as starting to get dressed. *This is crazy. I'm not related, and they're not going to let me see him anyway.* So instead, she tossed and turned with terrible thoughts running through her mind. She dreamed she was in the deep woods full of fog and thickets of thorn so dense she had to use arms and legs together to climb over and through them. She was searching for something, scrambling in slow motion, frightened for her life until she screamed one of those silent screams, those terrifying screams that take all your breath but make no sound. The silent scream woke her. *What was I looking for?* After she was more lucid, she realized what it was. *I think I was searching for what L.M. saw in the mirror. What could he have seen that was so awful? Was it his own death? Was it my death? The end of the world?*

Arnetta did something the next day she'd never done before. Right after lunch, she faked being sick. Walking into her class, she put her books down, put one hand to her stomach, and the other to her mouth, and ran out the door towards the bathroom. She made a few small retching noises on the way for good measure. After a few minutes, she washed her face with hot water, as hot as she could stand, making her face sort of a splotchy red. She tousled her hair, wiped her wet hands on her red blouse, and ambled back down the hall. The second bell rang just as she retrieved her books. She passed Mr. Suber, who gave her a nod after seeing her, and probably hearing from someone that she looked sick. She headed towards the nurse's office. *Just my luck, I probably really will get sick. My gag reflex was working on its own after I started faking it. Yuck. Thank goodness it never happened. One thing I hate is vomit.* Nurse Williams was at her desk when she arrived. Arnetta held one hand with crossed fingers behind her back as she pretended to adjust her book bag. "Hey, Mrs. Williams. I think I need to go home. I threw up this morning at home, but I thought that was it. I just threw up again, and I still don't feel too good, and now my stomach is starting to feel funny."

Mrs. Williams gave her a yellow slip of paper. "Here," she scribbled her official name, ripped it from a pad, and handed it to Arnetta, "Turn this into the teacher tomorrow, or when you can safely return to class. This will give you credit for a sick day and won't count as an absence. I hope you feel better, Arnetta. Do you need to call someone to pick you up?"

"Yes, Ma'am."

"OK. You can use the phone in there," Mrs. Williams pointed to the empty office next door. There was already another student waiting to enter her office.

Arnetta put her book bag on top of a desk with nothing on it but a phone, a clipboard full of stationery with the school's letterhead at the top, a pen, and an old typewriter. I *don't know if it's because I've never done this before, or because I'm hardly ever sick, or I'm just a good actress, but so far, this is pretty easy!* She dialed the number of the What's New shop 3-6-9-7-8-8-3. She'd memorized it because she'd joked with L.M. that the 7-8-8-3 could also spell S-T-U-F after he was so adamant that his shop didn't have just stuff, it must have been destined that way. *C'mon Brinda, pick up. I know we didn't plan this, but please pick up.* She didn't. She didn't pick up the next three times she tried either. *Where in the world are you, Brinda? Pick up the phone!* Arnetta returned the receiver to the phone. Looking around to see if Nurse Williams was watching, she was relieved to see her still busy with the other sick kid. OK, on to Plan B. She dialed another number.

199

CHAPTER NINETEEN

"Landreth High School? How can I direct your call?"

"Yes, I need to get an important message for a student. His name is Craig Walker, can you page him to come to the office?"

"Yes, Ma'am, I'll be glad to give him a message. Give me your name and number, and I'll have him call you back."

Uh oh. I wasn't expecting that. Hmmm. Think Arnetta, think. OK. "Well, you see, I'm calling from a borrowed phone, and as soon as I end this call, I'll be leaving for another location." *Well, at least part of that is true.*

"Well...I guess. I guess so, in that case, please hold the line."

Arnetta waited. She heard the announcement over the intercom.

Craig Walker, please come to the office.

She waited. And waited. *How long could it take to get someone to come to the office? What if this had been a real emergency.* Finally, she heard, "Hello?"

"Craig, hey, this is Arnetta, but..." she added in a hoarse whisper, "BUT DON'T SAY MY NAME, act like I'm your aunt or something. I need you to take me somewhere."

"Ok. Ok, Aunt Nettie, what's wrong?"

"Gosh Craig, I thought you were good in Drama class, dang, is that the best you could come up with? Aunt Nettie? Sorry. It's fine. I hate to do this to you, and I wouldn't ask if I didn't need you, but I kinda need you to leave school and take me to the hospital." Arnetta looked around to make sure she wasn't being watched or overheard. What she heard was Craig in a muffled whisper. He must've been trying to shield the phone with his hand to keep people on his end from eavesdropping.

"Are you sick? What's going on?"

Little did he know, she was only a couple of doors down from where he was standing. "No, Craig. It's not me. It's L.M. He's.... well, it's a long story. I'm supposed to meet Brinda to go see him after school, but I think I need to go now. I'll explain it all later. Can you take me?"

"Um, I guess so," then his voice got louder, "Yeah, I guess so. OK, Aunt Nettie, I'll be there in a few minutes. Tell Mom not to worry, I can take her to the doctor."

"Now, that's some drama, Craig. Thanks. I'll be outside by the gym, OK?"

"Ok, see you in a few."

Arnetta got back into her role as a sick student, turned around, thanked Nurse Williams with a single nod as she walked through the office door towards the gym.

"Arnetta?"

Uh oh. Busted. The hairs on her neck stiffened in high alert. Turning around at the speed of a ninety-year-old, she answered, "Yes, Ma'am?" *I hope my knees hold up; I may be sick for real this time.*

"I hope you feel better, honey. I looked at your record. You're never sick; hopefully, this is just a one-day bug, and you'll be back tomorrow."

Arnetta nodded her head in thanks and gave the ninety-year-old lady role another shot as she slowly raised her hand to wave good-bye. *Hey, if I pull this off, I may have to join Craig in Drama class. Romeo and Juliet, here we come.*

Arnetta stood by the gym entrance pretending to read the announcements. *As if I'd be interested in knowing the wrestling team's schedule.* However, the glass covering made a great mirror. Smiling as she saw the flash of a red car, she turns and does the ninety-year-old lady walk to the idling car. *You know, just in case anyone is watching.*

"What's going on, Arnetta?"

"Craig, something terrible happened late yesterday afternoon. You remember L.M. from the store yesterday, right?"

"Sure I do, why?"

"He almost died, he had a heart attack or something after you left. Brinda and I were still there, we had to call 9-1-1."

"Wow, Netta. That's wild. I've never seen anybody die or even come close."

"He's not dead yet, Craig, at least I hope not. He's in the hospital for goodness sakes. I want you to take me to see him. Can we go? Now?" *but I love that you called me Netta.*

"Oh, now I get it. I know where I fit into this picture."

OK, so he's smiling a little, but it's overshadowed by a different look. Worry? Exasperation? I hope he's not mad at me for having to leave school early. "Thank you, Craig."

"For what?"

"For this, for taking me. No, that's not it at all. For taking me, and for not even questioning when I called. You just came. I really appreciate it, thank you."

Craig's face lit up that time. His ears raised a little when he showed his full-face grin- Sonny Crockett would be proud, or rather Don Johnson playing Sonny Crockett would be proud.

They reached the hospital about one-thirty. Arnetta had a couple of hours before she was to meet Brinda at the front lobby entrance. *I hope I can see L.M. I really wanted to see him before Brinda gets here. I need to know what he saw in that mirror. It's not that I don't want her to know, but I think L.M. doesn't need us both bombarding with all kinds of questions. I hope he's OK, and I'm sure he needs to rest. It's not a case of he-was-my-friend-first, because, in truth, we all three met on the same day, just not physically. It's so complicated. I enjoy being with L.M. I enjoy being with Brinda too, it just seems awkward when it's the three of us.*

Craig went with her up to the sixth floor, where the cardiac care unit was. He stayed in the waiting room while Arnetta approached the nurse's station. After getting the ward secretary's attention, she asked where Mr. Mann was.

They didn't question her relationship to him, but she was told visits were limited to fifteen minutes, and only one visitor at a time while motioning to Room Four.

Arnetta walked on her tiptoes through the door but stopped when she saw L.M. lying there with his eyes closed. There's something very personal about a hospital room, but at the same time, it's very public. She found that very real in his room. *I've never been in a critical care room before; just about everything you wanted to know about his insides is being displayed on little beeping monitors.* He was almost completely covered up with a crisp white sheet, except for his arms. His hands had tape on them to hold some of the needles that allowed God knows what to be pumped into his veins. *Yuck! What's that? His pee?* It was his catheterization bag. *Well, I guess it's good to have one of those if you can't get out of bed. Poor L.M. Maybe I shouldn't be here, this is a little too persona...Oh, he's opening his eyes. He's going to be OK!*

L.M.'s eyes opened broader when he recognized Arnetta. "Hey you." He tried to direct her into the room closer, but his tethered arm stopped him. *He reminds me of Pinocchio, except those are tubes instead of puppet strings. All Pinocchio wanted was to be a real boy. I wonder what L.M. dreams about.* "L.M., you scared me half to death!" *OK, well, maybe not the best choice of words.* "You're going to be OK, right? We called 9-1-1 as fast as we could."

"Arnetta, it'll be OK. I will be OK. Not to worry. The paramedics said my granddaughters did everything just right, and if you hadn't acted as fast as you did, the outcome probably wouldn't be as good, as a matter of fact, I probably wouldn't even be talking to you right now. You saved my life."

"Granddaughters? Puleeze, L.M. You told them we were your granddaughters?"

"No, no, they just assumed that all on their own, but I didn't argue. I sort of like the idea." He tried to lace his fingers and rest his hands on his chest, but once again, those tubes wouldn't allow him the freedom. "Not that I'm old enough to be your grandfather, mind you."

Snickering while she pulled the one chair in the room closer to his bed, she sat down and physically changed her demeanor to all seriousness. *I know what he's doing. He's trying to make me feel comfortable in an uncomfortable circumstance. He's the patient, it should be the other way around.*

"L.M., I need to ask you some questions about the mirror." He clamped his eyes tighter than a clam above the tide line. *Is he in pain? Or is he just protecting that memory? Just like that clam, he's digging deeper into the sand.* "We can wait until later if you want, but I want to know what you saw."

Without moving his closed lids, he said, "I can't really explain what I saw Arnetta. I've never seen anything like it, and I've lived through a lot, let me tell you. It was an explosion that much I know for sure. But, as you know, we don't get to see the whole picture. I've gone over it in my mind all day. This is going to sound crazy, but here's what I saw. I saw a lady, a young lady with a bunch of children around her, I'm pretty sure she was a schoolteacher. All the children seemed to be about the same age...that part was sort of like a picture like it was posed, but then the lady stepped onto some kind of platform. It was a rocket ship; she turned and waved to the crowd, and then I saw the patch on her uniform, she was a NASA astronaut. It was an incredible thing to see! I couldn't help but feel awe, wonder, and admiration. It was like I was right there in the crowd. I was in the front row. The next part...the next part was godawful. There was an explosion." He opened his eyes, and tears rolled from the corners and fell to his pillow, "Arnetta, that rocket blasted off with a piece of the hearts of all the onlookers, and then it was just gone. Poof. Gone. Disappeared into thin air. But what I don't understand...it just doesn't make any sense, Arnetta, why would a schoolteacher...a...a regular person be going up in a spacecraft?" L.M. closed his eyes again and rocked his head back and forth against his pillow like he was pleading with his brain to disintegrate the memory.

"I didn't mean to scare you girls yesterday. I hadn't really been feeling all that well before you came." As if he had suddenly awakened from a long, restful sleep, his eyes popped open. He turned to Arnetta with a familiar brightness to his eyes, "Say, how is that fella you brought in to meet me yesterday at the store? He seems like a nice young man."

"He is." Arnetta felt the heat rising from her neck, hoping her face wasn't getting red. She pushed her glasses up on her nose as a distraction. "He's actually right outside, he brought me here. I'm supposed to meet Brinda downstairs about 3:30, but I really wanted to see how you were doing. Is there anything I can do for you, L.M.?"

"You've already done it, Arnetta. Just coming to see me is enough." Arnetta jumped when a buzzer went off, and then a tinny voice came over his room intercom. It was loud enough for the whole world to hear.

"Mr. Mann? You have a visitor. He said you were expecting him?"

"Yes, just a minute, please."

"Mr. Mann, you can only have one visitor at a time."

"OK. Just a minute, please."

After seeing that L.M. looked flustered, Arnetta offered, "Well, I guess I should go then."

"Oh, wait just a minute, Arnetta, he can wait a minute before he comes in." L.M. was fiddling with his hands again, making a temple with his fingertips. "Did you say you were meeting Brinda here this afternoon?"

"Yes. Between 3:00 and 3:30 in the lobby, then we're coming up here to see you." Arnetta stared at the intercom box, "I guess we'll come in one at a time, so we won't get you in trouble. Not to worry, we can take turns."

"You girls must've gotten your signals crossed. Brinda has already come and gone. She came this morning. I don't think she'll be coming back, Arnetta. She acted as though you and she had talked it through...she said she was going back home."

"Home?" Arnetta said it aloud, but it was meant mostly for her own ears. *Did Brinda mean home, like in going back to the What's New shop, or home, home, really back home, as in the home she left in such a hurry not too long ago?* Arnetta's hands were balled into fists, and her stomach was turning flip-flops, usually a pretty good indication that something wasn't right. Arnetta stood at the pace of a water-gushing geyser onto legs that were weak as water. "Oh yeah, how could I have forgotten that? Sometimes I can be such a dork, L.M. I better get going so your visitor can come in." Almost at the door, she turned back towards him, "You try to get some rest. I'll be back when I can. Oh, I forgot to tell you, we put a CLOSED UNTIL FURTHER NOTICE sign on the door at What's New, is that OK? Maybe when you're out of here, I can help you some, you know, after school. I'll be glad to, you know."

L.M. smiled, "Thanks, Arnetta. I'd like that very much. I really mean that. We'll talk later. Now, go on and be with that boyfriend of yours. Go grab a milkshake or something in the canteen downstairs."

"He's not my...." But L.M. was grinning big and shooing her out the door with his puppet-strung hands. Just a few steps outside his door, she passed someone. *Oh, that must be the man L.M. was expecting. Wonder who he is?* She watched him enter the room, *Hmmmm, probably not a preacher, he was carrying a briefcase, not a Bible.* As she passed the nurse's station, she had an idea. She turned around and waited for her turn while the secretary finished a phone call.

"Could I help you?"

"Yes, please. I feel like an idiot right about now. That man that just went into room Four? In my grandfather's room? Well, I know I know him plain as day, but I can't for the life of me remember his name, did he tell you his name by any chance?"

"No, he didn't."

"Oh, OK, well, thanks." But as Arnetta started toward Craig in the waiting room, the secretary called out to her.

"He didn't have to tell me his name, sweetie. We all know him. Don't you watch TV? He's a lawyer, maybe that's where you know him from." A middle-aged nurse with curls that surrounded her chubby face was standing behind the secretary and tried her best to sing the well-known jingle. *When you need justice, call Augustus. He's the man for you, call 555-22 22.* When she sang the 22 22 she used her fist like a gavel to knock on the desk with two short taps, then two more.

Arnetta nodded in recollection, "Oh, yeah! Sure, I have seen that commercial. Thanks. Catchy commercial, I knew I'd seen him somewhere." *Yeah. Augustus, 'Gus' Russell was the man in one of the corniest commercials ever. Gummy said he was an ambulance chaser. Why is he going to see L.M.? Later Sherlock, right now, you've got bigger fish to fry. Hopefully, Craig won't mind taking me to What's New to see what's new with Miss 'can't wait' Brinda.*

As Arnetta reached the waiting room, she glanced up at the clock and noticed it was almost two-thirty. *Brinda probably won't be expecting to hear from me until at least four o'clock. That would've been about the time I'd figured out she wasn't here and why.* She hadn't noticed she was standing in the doorway of the waiting room staring into space until she saw Craig spring to attention, tossing the car magazine down on the table littered with other periodicals.

"Everything OK, Netta? How's your friend?

"Oh, yes, thanks. I think he'll be OK. I'm afraid I need your help again, though, Craig. Are you up for it?"

Shoving his hands in his back pockets, he tucked his chin down a little, but then looked up through those thick lashes. *Ought to be against the law for guys to have lashes like that.*

"At your service Ma'am."

Am I dreaming? I'd pinch myself, but I guess that would be too obvious. Snap out of it Arnetta, you've got work to do.

"Where to?"

"We need to get to L.M.'s shop. I have a feeling Brinda's up to something. She may have skipped town on us. She's probably thinking I won't know anything for another hour or so because that's when I'm supposed to be meeting her. If we hurry, we may catch her."

On the way to the parking lot, Craig asked, "Where's she going?" and without waiting for an answer, he added, "Maybe it's for the best, Arnetta."

Arnetta looked at Craig like she was considering what he'd said. *I really didn't want Craig to know anything about the mirror connection between Brinda and me, and then she had to go blab her mouth. Not sure if it's because he might think I'm crazy, or he'd think I'm being petty and possessive. This past week, I'm the first to admit I've been a little stingy with L.M., the mirror, and even Craig. It's not like any of them belong to me, so why have I felt threatened I was losing any of them to Brinda? Am I going crazy?*

"Craig, I need to ask you a question."

"Shoot."

Arnetta slowed her pace, and asked, "When we were at the What's New shop yesterday. Did you *really* see a vision in the mirror?"

Craig stopped walking. He touched her elbow, making her turn towards him. "Are you serious?" He looked deeply into her questioning eyes, "You *are* serious, aren't' you? Arnetta, I was just playing with y'all. I think that guy, what's his name? Ellum?...or something like that. Anyway, I think he knew I was joking. I was just trying to set Brinda straight. I've met girls like her before, Arnetta. Like I said, maybe it's for the best."

Arnetta smiled and thought, *Craig, I sure hope you're real. I hope you don't self-combust or disappear in a vapor or anything.* They continued walking, Craig on the solid pavement, Arnetta on a cloud.

When they got to Craig's red Mustang, Arnetta had her hand on the door handle and realized she hadn't answered Craig's question about where Brinda may have been going. She looked over the roof of Bella, "Well, whether it's for the best or not, the least she could've done is say good-bye. You don't just leave." *I know from personal experience that some people do just leave. They leave and never come back, and they don't say good-bye.*

20

Covering Tracks

Craig and Arnetta pulled up in front of What's New. She could tell before even getting out that the store was empty. There were no lights on anywhere. She fished a keyring out of her purse and unlocked the front door. L.M. had already given Brinda his extra key when he'd told her she could spend the night there... *I meant to give the keys back to L.M. at the hospital, but now I'm glad I still have it. I figured he'd need it when he comes back, but we will probably have to depend on Craig again to get him back home and to the store.*

Craig opted to stay in the car to listen to the radio while Arnetta went inside to check on things. What's New always seemed dark, but today there was an eerie, foreboding element added. L.M. usually left a few lamps on, he'd said it made it look homey, but after bumping into a low coffee table, she knew another purpose for lighting. *I've never felt this kind of empty feeling in the store before, not with L.M. here.* It was a far off, but familiar feeling. The same feeling she had after she found out about her family's accident. A black hole. A void. Complete nothingness. As if on a mission, Arnetta went to every lamp and turned them on. As she walked by the vanity where they'd just been sitting near the day before, she noticed the mirror wasn't there. Brinda must've taken it to the office, or the room L.M. had offered her to sleep in. *I know I'm here all by myself, but for some reason, I feel like I'm trespassing, like someone else could be here.*

"Brinda? You in here?" no answer.

"Brinda?" *I just want to be sure if she's in the bathroom or something and didn't hear me call out. God forbid we run into each other and get the wits scared out of us, or worse, get a candlestick or something over the head in self-defense. There's a time and place for surprising people, but this wasn't one of them.* She walked all through the store, feeling each step like a deafening heartbeat until she finally reached the office, and then checked the bathroom and Brinda's room. She was nowhere to be seen, but what she found confirmed her suspicions about her new friend. On top of the upholstered chaise lounge, what was meant to be Brinda's makeshift bed, was an envelope. The envelope had Arnetta's name on it. She picked it up, turned it over, slid her thumb under the flap, and pulled out a single sheet of paper.

Arnetta,

I didn't want to leave without letting you know how much I enjoyed getting to know you. I wish things had worked out better. I know we've only known each other for a little while, but I feel like I've known you forever.

By now, you probably know I've taken the mirror with me. I think it's awfully painful for L.M. to have it anymore. I need to get back to my mom. She needs to look in the mirror too. I know she won't believe me when I tell her what I saw. I just hope she has the gift of sight like we do. Arnetta, I think my mom is in a dangerous place in her life. She needs the mirror more than anybody I can think of right now. Yes, even you.

I know how much you miss your mother. Please think about my mother and me for a minute. Nothing will bring your mother back, but the mirror will help me and my mom work things out between us and set her on the right track. I'm hoping the mirror will make her see the future isn't as hopeless as she thinks it is. I'm desperate to help her. If anything, even more so after meeting you, I realize I can't run away if there's a chance I can save her.

215

Arnetta, please don't be mad at me, and don't try to find me. I will tell you this, I started to take L.M.'s car but didn't want to be accused of stealing. All that is behind me now. I'll be all right, and you will be too. It's better if you don't know where I am. Maybe one day, we'll meet again. I hope so.
     Your friend,
     Brinda

Arnetta was standing the whole time she'd been reading but felt her body crumple to the chaise as she reread it. *What's going on here? What will I tell L.M.?* A lone tear escaped and fell to the hand-scribbled note. She wiped the wet spot from the page that had fallen on Brinda's name, causing it to smear. *That's just great. I seem to make everybody disappear. Nobody is safe around me.*

There was a light tap on the doorframe, causing her to jump. She reached underneath her glasses to wipe the other eye before another tear crawled down her face and turned to the doorway to see Craig.

"What's going on, Arnetta? No sign of Brinda, I see." He looked around the room and added, "What are you doing in here?"

"Just sitting." Arnetta folded the note and slid it into her jeans pocket while standing, "And thinking, I guess. I guess I'm trying to figure out what to do next."

"Well, for starters, let's say we get out of here and go grab a slice of pizza or something. I can take you home, or, if you'd like, you can come over to my house and watch a little TV? I'd offer to beat you in a game of Pac-Man, but I'm not sure if you'd like that or not."

"What, like playing Pac-Man? Or not like being beaten at playing Pac-Man? I'd love to play someday, but I'm not so sure about the-you-beating-me part, though."

"Ok. Challenge on. When do you want to play?"

"Not today. Hey, what time is it?"

Craig looked at his watch, "About three-thirty, why?"

"This day hasn't turned out at all like what I expected it to be. Craig? How about another kind of challenge?"

"What kind of challenge? You've already turned down Pac-Man." He walked closer towards her.

"Will you teach me how to drive?"

"You don't know how to drive?"

"Well, I do, but not really. I mean, I can drive a regular car, I guess, but not a stick shift. I took Driver's Ed just like everybody else. I even took a powder-puff mechanics course at the community college last year. I could check the oil, and maybe change a tire if I had to. But I've never really driven anywhere, there's been no need to, I don't have a car. Well, I take that back. I tried driving once in my Papaw's car. It's a stick shift, and, well, let's just say I don't do well with those."

"Mine's a stick too, ya know. What kind of car does your grandfather drive?"

"It's a 1969 Gran Torino. I bet it's never been over fifty miles per hour. They never go anywhere, but he's so protective of that car. He says it's got to last him forever. I think he's afraid if I drove it, I'd wreck it, or maybe take up racing or something."

Craig cocked his head and twisted his mouth in his best thinking pose.

Arnetta grinned, "Gummy always told me not to make a face like that, or it'd stick." Then she got serious, "Look, Craig. You don't have to. I know a boy's car is more valuable to him than anything else in the world. I know how much you love your Bella. It's OK. Really."

"Do you have a license?"

Fanning her face like Scarlett O'Hara, "Oh, do you have to have one of those? Oh my, I never even thought... Geez, Craig, how dumb do you think I am? Yes, I've got a license. I just don't have a car." She'd swatted his arm in a playful gesture. "I really haven't needed a car, they're expensive too, and with gas and insurance. I'd have to have more of a part-time job than babysitting to pull that off. I figured I'd have to get one when I go off to college."

"OK."

"OK?"

"Yeah, if you promise to be careful with my Bella, and not go ballistic with the least little thing, yes, I'll teach you to drive a stick shift."

"Girl Scout's honor." She held up her fingers in a salute. "I promise to take excellent care of Bella."

"I didn't know you were a Girl Scout, Netta."

"I'm not. It's just a figure of speech. I guess I could cross my heart and hope to die, stick a needle in my eye, but I can't guarantee safe driving with a needle stuck in my eye."

"Well, the needle only comes into play if you're lying. Man, you don't let up, do you?" The grin on his face told her he was only kidding.

"Ok, no joking around. No more car jokes. Let me lock up and turn off most of these lights and stuff. I'll be out in a few minutes. Be thinking about a good place for me to take a practice drive."

"All right, but let's just say drive, without the word practice. That makes me a little nervous. I'll see you by the car."

As soon as she heard the front door close, she zoomed back past L.M.'s office towards the back door. Opening the heavy door to the alley, she spotted L.M.'s car. It was the only thing there besides a couple of trash cans. *Sunbeam, thank goodness you're there, now let's see which one of these keys...Eureka! Thanks, L.M. for having all your keys on one* ring. *If his car wasn't a stick shift, I wouldn't need a lesson. All I need is a couple of hours of a refresher course, then I'll go home for a bite to eat, a nap until after the house is asleep, then I'm off on an adventure. I'm going on a road trip.*

21

Prophecy Revealed

The driving lesson went much better than Arnetta had hoped, and a million times better than Craig had feared. *I guess it really is true what they say about riding a bicycle, you never really forget.* Arnetta was evidently still glowing when Craig dropped her off precisely at five-thirty. Dropping her book bag on the end table by the green and brown plaid sofa, she walked into the kitchen where her grandmother was finishing up supper.

"Hey, Gummy."

"Hey yourself, Arnetta," taking the time to turn away from stirring her brew of sweet tea, "You sure are chipper this evenin.'"

"I guess I am, aren't I?" Arnetta sauntered over to the oven and cracked open the door to get a preview of the menu. "Yummm!" she closed her eyes and put a hand to her stomach, "I thought I smelled chicken pot pie! It looks like it's almost ready, I'll set the table."

Gummy's chicken pot pie was another one of Arnetta's favorite foods. Since Gummy retired, she seemed to take more time to experiment with new foods, so Arnetta was glad when the old favorites hit the menu. Some of her epicurean tests didn't go over so well with Arnetta and Papaw, like the time she followed a recipe in McCall's magazine for chicken Coq-au-vin. Gummy didn't take too kindly to Papaw, saying he preferred his fried chicken saying cock-a-doodle-do rather than some little whiny chicks getting drunk and swimming around in alcohol. Arnetta had read the recipe and laughed out loud when he punned whiny chicks even though she wasn't sure he knew he'd meant it as a pun. Gummy tried to talk over the laugh, explaining that she'd read vin, the wine part, was what made it a special dish. She hadn't prepared it again, and even Gummy ended up laughing a bit as they finished off the whiny chicks.

Breezing back into the kitchen to fill the glasses with ice, Arnetta broached the road trip topic, "Gummy, I forgot to tell you about a field trip our class is taking. I hope it's OK, but I went ahead and signed up for it today. Today was the deadline. I sort of forged your signature on the permission slip."

Gummy turned around and gazed at her granddaughter with a keen squint of wariness. She was wearing her favorite apron, the one with the red cardinals all over it, and ruffles on the shoulder, and was holding a head of lettuce in one hand and her favorite sharp knife in the other. That knife had done so much cutting, it was worn in the middle. It was as thin as the hair was getting on Papaw's head. Arnetta had caught her right at the beginning of making a salad. "Now Arnetta, you know how I feel about these kinds of things. Not just that you forged my name, but school trips in general. Where is it your class is going that it's so important for you to go, but not important for me to know nothing about?"

"Gummy, please don't be mad. I told you I forgot. I've been busy with science class lately. I just forgot about it. I wasn't trying to keep it from you. I can catch up on any chores when I get back. It's my political science class. We leave in the morning." *I feel like I need to be hopping around so those lightning rods can't catch me. I hate spinning this web of lies, but...*

"In the morning? I'd say you forgot! I'm not mad, Arnetta, it's just what in the world am I going to do with you? I won't be around forever to look after you, you know. You've got to start taking some responsibility. And you say you're leaving in the morning? Well, at least you won't be missing your studies, I'll have to give that one to the school, a weekend trip. Where to? Where are you going?"

"Washington?" *Ohhh, I didn't mean it like the question it came out with. I guess I didn't realize how crazy it sounded that such a big trip like Washington could have been forgotten. Why did I pick Washington? Oh yeah, Columbia, the state capitol was my first choice, but I needed an excuse for an overnight trip in case I'm delayed finding Brinda. Yes. Washington, it is.*

Arnetta could tell she had Gummy's attention as her grandmother wiped her hand on a dishtowel, and then slapped it back across her shoulder. Her eyes were boring a hole right through Arnetta. "Washington? Which Washington? There's a Washington, GA, a Washington, NC, a Washington, DC..."

"That one."

"Which one?"

"Washington, DC. We'll be leaving at about five o'clock in the morning." *I better start working on a plan B in case this doesn't work. I'm not sure she's buying it.* Then she remembered how much Gummy hated paperwork, she complained about it all the time. How many times had she heard Gummy say, 'That school should spend more time teaching than wasting paper all the time. "I'm sure there was something about this trip in the packet of information from the beginning of the year, remember seeing anything? It seems like I remember you saying you had to sign your life away just to get me in the Eleventh grade." *I think it's working.* "Want me to try and find it for you?"

"No, no. I've probably thrown most of that stuff out by now." Gummy sighed out loud. "Well? I guess that's it then."

"What I thought about doing was, after supper, of course, packing my things, and then I'd go over to Amy's house. She wanted me to stay over there so we could make sure we get up on time to be at the school by 4:45. That's what time the line-up is, and you know Mr. Adair, he doesn't put up with tardy."

Since there was no reply, Arnetta took that as a yes. She hated lying to Gummy, though, and she felt it in the pit of her stomach. *I don't really have a choice, do I? I've got to find Brinda and bring the mirror back to its rightful place.*

"Gummy, if it's all right with you, I'm going to eat in my room. That way, I can be getting my things together while I'm savoring your chicken pot pie." *And I won't have to look at you in the eyes during dinner, because I know you'd see the deceit in mine.*

"Arnetta, you just won't do." Gummy walked over to Arnetta. She had pulled the pot pie out of the oven, and now her hard-working arms rested around Arnetta's shoulders. *I can smell the yeast from the buttery crust she put on top of the pot pie. Gummy loves me in a different way than my Mama did, and cooking for Papaw and me is just one of those ways, I guess.* "Well, come on then, let's serve your plate." She'd released the hug, but held Arnetta at arm's length, "Do you need a little spending money, Arnetta? I know you'll want to buy a souvenir or two."

"Um...Yes, Ma'am, sure. But you don't have to..."

Gummy walked over to her coffee canister, "I know I don't have to, Arnetta. Here." And she handed over some folding money, as Gummy called it. Arnetta didn't look at the bills for a count as she shoved them into her jeans pocket.

Arnetta fixed her plate, trying not to look like a pig. She retrieved her glass from the table and added more ice because the tea was still warm. Balancing her fork, napkin, and tea in one hand, and the plate full of creamy goodness in the other, she pushed open the swinging door- that went from the kitchen to the den-with her foot.

Papaw was in his recliner watching the nightly news. He refused to buy a hearing aid, so when the TV was on, it was blasting loud enough for the whole neighborhood to hear whether they wanted to or not. Arnetta smiled at him as she strolled past the TV on her way to the stairs.

There are moments in your life when something happens, and everything seems to go in slow motion, sort of like you're watching it happen instead of it happening to you. Why is that? Is it because our minds are trying to make it better to understand what's happening? Arnetta was having one of those moments. *I'm aware of my legs moving, I'm walking towards the stairs. I'm aware of the smile and the angle of my head as I'm sending thought waves of love to Papaw sitting in his recliner. I'm aware of my hair flying around as I turn my head back toward my path. I'm aware of the extremely loud TV news broadcast. Is Papaw going deaf? Wait...What? I forced myself to turn back towards the TV as George H.W. Bush is doing an interview with the newscaster.*

The Vice President is talking about the space program. There's a little picture of a woman, a history teacher. Her name is Christia McAuliffe, and she will be the first civilian in space next year. It's a joyous moment, everyone is smiling. The newscaster, the Vice President and the face of the history teacher in the corner of the screen. What happens next is what happens when the slow motion of a moment crashes into the here and now. Arnetta stopped in mid-stride, her stomach lurched into one complete knot. The glass and utensils slipped from her hand. *Oh no!* While trying to catch the glass from falling from one hand, the plate full of food tumbled to the linoleum floor and crashed, sending chards of the plate and chicken pot pie all over the floor and the wall.

Gummy came running from the kitchen, following the same path Arnetta had taken. First, she started towards Papaw, probably assuming he had fallen or something. Papaw hadn't even turned around; either the volume was so loud he didn't hear, or he was mesmerized with what was on the TV.

"Arnetta? What happened?"

I look at my clothes, saturated with sweet tea and goo, I look at the wall and baseboard covered with the same goo now trailing down like tears. "Gummy, I'll get it. I'm sorry. I'm so sorry. I must've slipped on something." *But I know. I know whatever I slipped on wasn't on the floor.*

"Oh, go fix yourself, and then come down and get another plate. I'll get it. Go on now." Gummy scooted Arnetta off with her hands.

Gummy and Arnetta looked over at Papaw. *He's clueless, and just as well. He loves chicken pot pie as much as me, and if he'd seen the mess on the floor, he probably would be telling me about all the starving children all over the world that couldn't eat Gummy's chicken pot pie... Not sure how my plate of food all over the floor would help the hungry but thank goodness I'm spared this time.*

"Thank you, Gummy. I'm so sorry. I'll be right back down."

Arnetta obeyed and feeling every bit of sorry as she did. She went to the bathroom, grabbed a washcloth and soaked it, and tucked a couple of dry hand towels under her left arm, then she retrieved her book bag and held it at a distance so as not to get it messed up, and ran up the stairs. Although most of the food had ended up on the floor, plenty was soaking into her clothes. Stripping down to her bra and panties, she used a hand towel to get the food off, then saturated them with the wet washcloth, and attempted to dry them with the other hand towel. *These are my favorite jeans, too, great Arnetta. Just great.* Try as she might remove any evidence of her accident, knowing as hard as she tried, it was nothing compared to what else she was facing. She studied herself in the dresser mirror. *Well, Arnetta, it looks like you'll be going to Washington after all.* Her eyes dropped to her chest as if she'd be able to see her skin move to the beat of her heart, *it feels like it's getting ready to pop right out. I guess I'd never really thought about my road trip past Cherokee. I've got to find Brinda, and maybe I'll find her along the way, but if what L.M. saw in the mirror can be stopped...I have to try. If it can be prevented, that history teacher and the astronauts won't have to die.*

She finished cleaning herself up, and went back down-stairs, stopping off in the bathroom room to deposit the dirty things in the laundry hamper. Her nose picked up the Pine-Sol smell long before she saw everything had been cleaned up. She got herself a small bowl and fixed herself a half-portion, feeling guilty for taking any at all.

Gummy was just now fixing her and Papaw's plates. Arnetta told her again how sorry she was, Gummy just nodded while continuing to dish out supper. Papaw came shuffling into the kitchen and started one of his one-sided conversations.

"They gone send another spaceship up there next year, Bessie. You know what that means, we gone have more bad weather. They gone take a schoolteacher up there this time." He turned his gaze to Arnetta, "Guess you can't ever get done with school, Arnetta. You best pay attention to your studies. Look at them astronauts, they didn't pay attention, now they gotta take a teacher up there to catch them up on their studies." He grinned at his own corny joke, all the time watching ladles of chicken potpie being dumped onto his plate.

Arnetta smiled and slipped behind him to head back upstairs.

22

Road Trip - Day One

After Arnetta had eaten, she went back downstairs to take her bath. She grabbed her new toothbrush and the sample size toothpaste she'd gotten from the dentist's office, roll-on deodorant, and a couple of washcloths. Returning to her room, she pulled down her tote bag from the closet shelf and packed a few necessary items for her road trip. *OK, what am I going to need? This is like going camping, not that I've ever been camping before. I have no idea. Just put it in there, if I don't need it, it's OK. Better to have it and not need it than need it and not have it.* In addition to the toiletries, she packed her hairbrush, panties, sleep bra, a nightshirt, a couple of her favorite neon T-shirts, a pair of jeans, and after a minute of deliberation, her Members Only jacket and paisley neckerchief. She pictured herself standing face-to-face with President Reagan and felt a smile tug at her lips because she'd thought enough of him to wear her dress-up jacket. *If I wear it, I'll have to tuck in my T-shirt since it's longer than the jacket.* She usually wore the hip-length shirt pulled up on one hip and tied off with a hair tie, just like all the other girls, but not for the President. She stuffed her tracksuit in the tote, and barely got her high-top Keds and socks in there before struggling with the zipper to close. It wouldn't. *Hmmm. I know, I'll use my bookbag, why not? She unpacked and started over, this time putting the toiletries, flashlight, and sleepwear in the book bag. Much better. Now for the fun part.*

The quickest way to get back to town would be to hop on her bike, but she hadn't realized how much stuff a *few* things would be. She slung her book bag over both shoulders, something she rarely did. *I know I'll look like a dork, but maybe no one will see me as late as it is.* She pulled the long straps of the tote over her head and left shoulder and rested the bulk underneath her elbow. After a few steps of getting her balance, she was ready to go.

The timing was right on target as it was just past ten o'clock, and Gummy and Papaw had already retired for the evening. Arnetta had already pulled her bike loose from the bungee cords holding it to the porch railing earlier so she wouldn't create too much noise. It was wobbly steering at first, but after she got her weight shifted, it was hunky-dory. *I've never been on my bike this late before. A little scary but exhilarating at the same time. The night air is cold and damp, but the closer I get to town, it's getting warmer and warmer. I don't know if it's me, because I'm warming up, or if the streetlights can put off that much heat. It was cold when I went over the bridge.* The amber glow from the streetlights cast eerie shadows but created a sanctuary as it flooded the streets with its artificial sepia tones.

When she reached the What's New shop, she got off her bike and walked it through the alley that led to the back of the store. She nearly jumped out of her skin as a cat jumped down from a garbage bin. *Geez, get with it Arnetta, it's just a cat. If that's going to spook you, you may as well turn around right now.* Just as that negative thought tried to make itself comfortable, a more positive one kicked it to the curb, *pull it together, we must do this. This is for L.M., and, who knows? This may be a matter of national security!* She smiled as she envisioned President Reagan awarding her the Medal of Honor.

After reaching the back of the store, she was glad to get to L.M.'s car. Her driving lesson fresh in her mind boosted her confidence. Thinking of Craig didn't hurt either. After leaning her bike against the building, she started towards the car, but flung herself back and plastered herself as flat as she could against the building when a bright white light shone down the dark alley. *What the heck?* She leaned her head out just a smidge to see a police car cruising on patrol. *Gosh, that was close.* Listening until she heard nothing, she continued towards the car. *The streets of Landreth are dead as a doornail at night. I don't know if I should feel safe or* scared. I think half the battle will be getting out of this town without being stopped. I feel like a cat burglar.

Arnetta retrieved the keys from her pocket and unlocked the door. She tossed the book bag into the passenger seat, leaned in, and unloaded the heavy tote to the back seat. She rubbed a spot on her shoulder where the straps had started to burn and then moved her neck from side to side to pull out the numbness. She stopped turning when her eyes landed on her bike, where it stood leaning against the brick building. *I wonder...* After opening the trunk, she wrestled with the cumbersome bike, but after some finagling, turned the bike's handlebars backward to make it fit inside the trunk.

Getting into the driver's seat took almost as much maneuvering as her bike. *If I could just fold myself up...* Looking down at her feet on the floorboard. *Oh, I forgot about those.* The foot pedals, custom made for L.M.'s short legs, reached about mid-calf on Arnetta's legs. *This reminds me of the time I tried to show Benji how to ride his tricycle, my knees were up towards my face.* It took a minute, but she finally figured out how to adjust the seat further back and still reach the steering wheel. She thought of L.M. *What kind of life he must have, he needs to modify everything to fit his small frame?* Locking the doors, she stuck the key in the ignition, but before starting the engine, she slumped back into the seat. Arnetta bowed her head. *Dear God, please protect me as I go about my mission to help others. Please let me be doing the right thing. In Jesus' name. Amen. Starting the car with one foot on the brake and the other on the clutch.* The stick was pulled into the R slot while gradually pulling her foot off the clutch just the way Craig showed her. Chug, chug, nothing. After a couple of tries, she was successful and started inching her way back through the narrow, dark alley. *I sure don't want to scratch this car, and this is tighter than a gutter ball at the bowling alley.* Backing out onto Collier Street, she felt the tension release from her shoulders. *Well, if backing up is the hard part, I've got it made for a while.*

After a few minutes of driving, Arnetta pulled into a 7-11. She had the money Gummy had given her in her pocket but still hadn't looked to see how much was there. She also had some money she'd taken from her savings jar in her room. Arnetta knew she had at least a hundred dollars in there, but she had only taken the paper money and left the change. She sat in the car for a minute, trying on her 'big girl look' in the rear-view mirror. *If somebody asks me why I'm out so late or something, I've got to make it look like it's no big deal. Besides, kids are out a lot later than this on game nights.* All she needed was a map, but she got a Cherry Coke Slushee, some chips, and chewing gum too.

Back in the car, she threw the bag in the passenger seat and slurped a few draws from her Slushee before positioning the cup between her legs. *I wish L.M.'s car had one of those cup holder things. He probably never eats or drinks in here, though, so he hadn't thought about it.* She thought about getting the map out but changed her mind when she noticed the store clerk looking her way. *That's OK. I know the general direction I'm going; I'll just wait until I get to a well-lit pull off or something.* She buckled her seat belt, made a show of adjusting her mirror, checking her side mirrors, and backed out of the parking space without a hitch. *Piece of cake.* She didn't stop until she got to Highway 11, because it was just too dark. After a few minutes, she spotted a gas station with a couple of big trucks in the lot. *That's a great place to check my map. It's a good thing I don't need gas yet because this place looks pretty seedy with all those half-lit neon beer signs blinking. I'm glad they leave their lights on, I better pull up close to the station so I can see the map better.* Something out of the corner of her eye caught her attention. *What? Could that be…Brinda? Sure looks like her.* The person she saw didn't look identical to Brinda, but it had to be. The girl sort of stumbled from the back of the building. It looked like she was sleepwalking. She was headed towards an 18-wheeler with its cab door open. *What? What in the world are you doing? I've got to do something.*

236

Arnetta jerked open her car door, and yelled, across the top of the car

"Brinda? Hey, Brinda!"

Brinda whipped around, startled to hear someone call her name.

Me and you both, Brinda.

Trying to think faster than her brain wanted her to, Arnetta added, "Hey Brinda, come 'ere! I've got something to show you, you're not going to believe this!" She saw Brinda hold her index finger to the truck and started walking towards Arnetta.

When Brinda got within five feet of the BMW, she said, "Arnetta? What are you doing here?" She opened the passenger door, "This is L.M.'s car, right? Man, what are you doing out here this time of the night?"

Arnetta was already back behind the wheel and buckled in. "Brinda, get in. I've got to tell you something."

"What?"

"Just get in."

Brinda sighed and looked back toward the truck as if trying to decide.

Come on, Brinda, just get in.

Finally, Brinda slid in the passenger seat, and tossed her tote bag in the back seat, clutching her backpack in her lap. Arnetta could see the handle of the mirror sticking out of the side opening.

"Brinda, have you been drinking? I can ask the same thing of you, what are you doing out this time of night?"

"Just trying to get home, Arnetta." Brinda rested her head against the car window, "Just trying to get home."

Arnetta glanced over at the truck. The cab door was still open. "And that truck? I guess the truck driver was going to take you there. Is that it?"

Brinda righted herself. "I thought you wanted to show me something. What is it?"

With that, Arnetta started the car and took off, making the tires squeal as she got back on the highway.

"What are you doing, Arnetta? Where are we going?"

"Just take it easy, Brinda. Take it easy and listen."

They drove in silence for a few seconds before Arnetta told Brinda about what she'd seen on the TV. She revealed to Brinda her plans to come find her. Well, her and the mirror. But now, the purpose wasn't to take her back to Landreth. No, now they were on a mission, and it may take both of them to pull it off.

"Brinda, have you ever been to Washington?"

"Washington? You mean like DC?

"Why does everybody keep saying that? Yes. Washington, DC"

"No, I haven't, and... I haven't lost anything...there either, so I don't ... need to go 'find' anything there, so why...?"

Arnetta stole a couple of quick glances at Brinda. *Why is she talking so slow?* "Brinda, are you on something?

"No, why?" Brinda adjusted herself and sat up straighter in the seat. "I'm just tired. Very tired. Think I'll just take a little na...Arnetta! Look out!" Brinda had shouted, but Arnetta had seen the look on her face before her words had come out, making her turn her eyes back to the road just in time to see a deer inches from the car.

Arnetta slammed on the brakes, causing the car to spin a little to the left, almost slamming into the deer again as it darted to safety. She could see the whites of the deer's eyes, sheer panic. *I wonder if that deer saw the same look of terror in my eyes.* The car stalled. Craig's rule number three popped into her head. *Always remember to use the clutch when you apply the brakes.* Saying out loud, but more to herself than to Brinda, "Mark my words, I will never own a car with a stick shift." Arnetta tried to start the car. "Luckily, there's no one on the road but us. That's the good news." She tested the ignition again. "The bad news?" Still not starting. "There's no one on the road but us." Whatever had Brinda so out of it earlier had vanished, and she was wide awake.

"Arnetta, here, let me try. I can drive awhile. That deer got you pretty shook up. Me too, but I'm awake now. That was a big one. It could've totaled the car for sure."

Arnetta looked at Brinda with a cynical look of disbelief, and even though she didn't say it out loud, Brinda probably got the thought waves she was sending. *Oh yeah. I'll let you drive because you're just so good at driving, aren't you? You only totaled a car, um, oh yeah, less than a week ago?* Arnetta rolled her eyes and shook her head, then she unlocked the car door, unbuckled her seat belt and stepped out into the chilly night air.

The girls passed each other at the rear end of the car. The same thought must have passed through their minds at the same time. They both smiled and said in unison 'stoplight fire drill,' but of course, there was no stoplight, and there was no hurry since they were in the middle of nowhere in the middle of the night.

Brinda got the car started on the first try. "I think you flooded it. It just needed to recover." Her shoulders slumped, and she gave a heavy sigh before continuing. "I feel like I need to explain." She pulled the car back into the right lane and proceeded on their journey. "I'm sorry for leaving without saying goodbye, well, except for the note. I just decided to go see L.M. a little earlier than what we'd planned because I felt the need to get to my mother. The images I saw in the mirror were so strong, they gave me a sense of urgency; it's almost like every second counts."

"What do you think about what L.M. saw?"

"Huh?"

"What L.M. saw before he had the heart attack? Did y'all talk about it?"

"Um, no. I didn't want to upset him. That was some scary stuff, he could've died!"

"I know. It must have been terrifying for him, and I don't think he's out of the woods yet, you know? He looked sort of weak when I saw him, but I think he wanted to tell me, tell someone anyway. As he was recounting what he saw, I could still see the terror in his eyes. It must've been like the worst nightmare imaginable. I've never really seen terror like that, you know? And now, I've seen it three times in less than 48 hours."

"Three times?"

"Yes. In L.M.'s eyes, when he saw the vision the first time, in the hospital when he was telling me about it, and that deer, you saw his eyes, right? That must be the look you have when death is imminent."

"Yes, I saw the deer's eyes. That was weird. Like I said, every second counts, and you and that deer only had milliseconds to react. I guess we were all lucky."

"Brinda, do you believe in luck? Sometimes I think life is like drawing straws, sometimes you get the long one, and sometimes you get the short one."

After that, things got very quiet. It felt better to be silent than fill the air with chitchat. Arnetta felt her eyelids getting heavy. She thought about terrorized eyes and couldn't help but wonder about her family. *How many milliseconds did they have?* The very idea forced a tear to slide down her cheek as she squeezed her eyes shut to escape the thought. *Where was the mirror then? What if someone could've seen a warning of their accident and somehow stopped it from happening? I guess I got the short straw. No one would understand if I told them, and most people would argue that I got the long straw because I got to live, but it sure doesn't feel that way. That's why I've got to see if we can stop another accident from happening. I'm so sleepy. Just a little snooze won't hurt.*

Brinda ended the silence, "Hey, Arnetta. I think I'm going to have to pull over and stretch my legs a bit. You can drive if you want. I'm tired, and I'm afraid I'll go to sleep at the wheel."

No answer. "Oh Arnetta, I know you've only had about a thirty-minute nap, and I hate to disrupt that peaceful look, but I've got to find a place and grab a few winks myself. All I see is trees. I'll just keep going a bit farther. Just a quiet out-of-the-way place with no houses around, a place we can sort of be tucked away from the road." A few minutes later, "Aha! Here it is. A state park road. This will be our room for the night. This little dirt road is perfect, and there's a small opening. Perfect." Brinda looked over at Arnetta as she turned off the ignition. She was still sleeping, but Brinda continued her conversation as if she were awake, "Arnetta, I wish you could see the moon, it's beautiful. Never mind, we both need sleep." Brinda checked to be sure the doors were locked, climbed over the car seat, pushing her and Arnetta's tote in the floorboard. She folded her hands in a prayer pose and used them as a pillow underneath her face. It didn't take long for her to join Arnetta in slumberland.

23

Road Trip - Day Two

Arnetta woke up in the passenger seat of the car. It took a minute to register that she was in L.M.'s car. Alone. *Where is Brinda?* Looking around, she saw her answer piled up in a fetal position in the back seat. Arnetta yawned, then made smacking sounds as she tried to clear away some of the morning mouth. *I remember Gummy telling me more than once, 'Morning mouth is a lot like a herd of elephants trampled through there while you were sleeping. There may be one of two left in there, you best go brush your teeth.' Thanks, Gummy. You have a way with words.* Arnetta pulled her hand to her neck to massage the kink formed from sleeping in an odd position. She removed her glasses and rubbed the sandman doodoo out of the corner of her eyes and checked her Mickey Mouse for the time. *Almost seven o'clock.* Looking out the window, she saw the sun peeking above the horizon of a lake. Well, isn't that beautiful? I don't know where we are, but at this very moment, I don't care. But, by the next moment, realization set. *I'm not on vacation, we have a mission to complete.* And another, even more, timely realization. *First things first, I've got to pee.*

She unbuckled her seat belt and unlocked her door with care as to not wake Brinda. *Who knows how long she's been out? An hour? Several hours? There's a tree. I hope I can do this. I've never really mastered the art of peeing in the woods with your clothes on. Not exactly something they teach in Home Economics class.* After rising from her squat, she zipped up her jeans and stretched. *If it's one thing I can do well, it's stretching.* Another Gummyism popped into her head. *How many times have I heard her say, 'I'd stretch a mile if I didn't have to walk back.'* That always made Arnetta smile, but today the thought of Gummy brought remorse instead. *I shouldn't have lied to Gummy the way I did. But she would've never understood. It's probably better that she doesn't know I'm out here in a stolen car with a girl I hardly know. A fugitive. Yeah, it's also better she doesn't know about the mirror or that her granddaughter is seeing things, or that same granddaughter is headed to Washington DC to try and put a stop to something that hasn't even started yet. That's what she'd say. I can almost hear her now, "Hogwash, Arnetta! Stop this foolishness! You better get your head out of them clouds; that imagination of yours is going to get you in a heap of trouble!" Yeah. This time, I think it's OK to have conjured up that little white lie,* she walked over to another tree, and after another stretch, squatted and sat back down on her haunches with her arms crossed over her knees. *I feel dirty. I'd love nothing more than to go jump in that lake.*

"There you are, I wondered where you were."

Arnetta stood up faster than she knew she could. "Gosh, you scared me. Where are we, do you know?

"Well, I did drive us here, you know. But no, not really, I don't know where we are exactly. I was just getting so sleepy, I had to pull over. It's not that far back up to Highway 11. I'm ready to get back on the road whenever you are."

"OK. I'm ready." Both girls walked back towards the car, "Pretty soon, I need to get something to eat. I didn't have much last night, how about you?"

"Yeah. Ate a little at that little trucker gas station. Wait, were you there while I was eating? How'd we hook up?"

"I knew it! You were acting really funny last night, Brinda. When I saw you, you were getting ready to hop into an 18-wheeler,"

"Oh. That was Jimmy. He offered to take me up the road a bit."

Understanding seemed to hit Brinda's face at the same time Arnetta said, "Right."

"Arnetta, thank you." Her eyes still wide, "I'm not sure, but you may have just saved my life. You must be my guardian angel; you keep showing up when I need you."

"I'm no guardian angel, Brinda, but you're welcome. I think it's called a gut feeling. You should try to listen to yours more. "

"No, it's a gift. I think you have the power of premonition."

"What, you mean like ESP?

"Yeah, something like that."

"No. I think my "power," Arnetta used air quotes, "Is just a feeling I have in my gut. It's nothing more than the fight-or-flight response everyone has. I've always been on hyper-alert, well, since my family's accident, but I still think everyone has the ability."

Reaching the car, Arnetta opens the door and leans in instead of getting inside.

"What are you doing?"

"I'm looking for the map."

"What map?"

"I bought a map at the 7-11, just before I ran into you. I'd only stopped to read the map when I saw you."

"Oh. I think I may have stuck it under my seat." Brinda got in the car and fished around underneath her seat, "Here. Here it is. Sorry. I guess I moved it so I wouldn't sit on it."

"That's OK. I just want to check to see which road to get on next, looking at this map, it looks like we may need to backtrack a little. *Gosh, who knew all these roads were here. They really ought to teach map reading in school.* "This reminds me of those maze puzzles you follow along with a pencil." *I was never any good at those.* "Hopefully, as long as we're going north, northeast, we should be OK. If we get to a dead-end, we'll have to backtrack. That's why it's good to have two people, right? One to drive, and one to look at the map and navigate."

The rest of that day was spent driving, learning more about each other, singing to the radio and wondering what kind of people lived in the towns they passed through. They stopped for bathroom breaks and snacks. As they neared Washington, they found a Motel 6 and checked in. The huge roadside sign stated $18.95 Clean Rooms and Free TV. It was getting close to nine o'clock when they pulled into the parking lot.

Once inside, the first thing Brinda does is flip on the TV, and collapses spread-eagle across one of the two double beds, with the remote control in her hand. Arnetta goes to the bathroom and turns on the shower.

"I'm going to take a shower; I'm feeling a little grimy."

"OK, I'll go next. Take your time, I'll just watch some TV."

Arnetta thought about being frugal with hot water, the way she had to be at home. She closed her eyes and let her thoughts drip down her body along with the steamy drops. *These motels need to have a lot of water heaters, I guess. I could stay in here forever.* After washing her hair with the tiny bottle of shampoo provided, she rinsed and turned the water off. Grabbing two towels, she wrapped her hair in a turban with one, and covered herself with the other one, high up under her arms, and tucked the end to free her arms to open the door. "It's all yours, Brinda." Stepping out into the now cold room, she couldn't see a thing because her glasses were steamed up, but the TV was on, and she heard a rerun of I Dream of Jeannie. She used the bottom of her towel to wipe her glasses. *I always loved that show.* "Brinda?" The bed was empty. Panic started to set in. *If she has run off again...the car...the mirror...*Arnetta ran to the door and jerked it open. The first thing she saw was L.M.'s car parked right in front of the door; the next thing was Brinda rambling up the walkway with a bucket of ice in her hands.

"Arnetta? What's the matter? You look like you've seen a ghost. I'm not sure you should be standing here dressed, or rather undressed like that." Brinda slipped past Arnetta through the doorway. Arnetta still had her hands on her hips.

"Don't do that."

"Do what?"

"Don't just leave, Brinda."

"Sor-reee, I just went to get some ice, you were in the shower, so you wouldn't have heard me anyway."

"Sorry. I just...well, it's been a long day, I guess. Guess it's my turn to watch a little TV, huh?"

249

"Yeah. Here, we can split a Coke. I would've gotten two, but they want fifty cents apiece!"

"Thanks, Brinda. That'll hit the spot."

Brinda fixed her drink over ice and took it into the shower. Arnetta changed into her sleep clothes and settled on her bed to watch some of the I Dream of Jeannie show. *Imagine having your own magic bottle with a Genie, ready to grant any wish you had. That astronaut, Capt. Tony Nelson doesn't know how good he has it...or, does he? Here he has the world at his command, and he doesn't seem to want it. It's sort of like the mirror in a way. The mirror can show you the future, and in some ways, that could become a moneymaker, and not just a little money either. A magic bottle would instantly grant you what you want, but it seems like in all the tales I've ever read or seen in movies, at least one of those three wishes backfired. Can that happen with the mirror too? What if this whole trip fails? What if the vision wasn't real? What if we can't get a message to the President? What if...*

Brinda busted out the bathroom door, naked as a jaybird. "Man, it's hot in there." She sprinted over to her bed and got under the covers.

"You're naked."

"Yeah? So what?"

"You're weird."

"Did I ever tell you about the time...?" Brinda went on and on and on. Either the shower or the Coke, or both energized her like she'd had a full night's sleep. She talked about her family, different legends, the mirror, and more. *I thought I'd heard her tell just about every Indian story she knew on the car ride, but I was very mistaken. The one that's really glued to my mind is the tale of Spearfinger. The look on her face as she recited it was as horrible as the story itself. Something about the way she told it made it seem very real.*

The Legend of Spearfinger

Long, long ago, there lived a strong medicine woman named Spearfinger. She was a shapeshifter and could take on any given shape at any given time. Her physical appearance was that of an old woman, but her skin was so rough and hardened by the elements, that it looked like stone. Another name for her was *Nun wum wi*, which meant 'dressed in stone.' On her right hand, her forefinger was very long and bony, that's how she got the name Spearfinger. She was such a strong woman that she could lift heavy stones and fuse them together just by hitting them against each other. She would travel over the mountain ranges, and sometimes sit at the top of the mountains and observe all the people below.

Over the years, she managed to build a stone bridge all the way from Hiawassee, GA to Whiteside Mountain, between Highlands and Cashiers, North Carolina. Spearfinger had an appetite for livers—human livers. She would entice children to wander from their villages by calling to them by singing a lovely tune. When the children got close enough, she would grab them and using that long bony finger, tear out their livers and eat it right there in front of them. They wouldn't object, because they were under her spell. Her finger was so sharp, the puncture hole was barely noticeable. The children, no longer under her spell, would return to their village only to die a few days later.

After losing many children over the years, several of the chiefs from different villages had a big meeting, and it was decided they would form a group to kill Spearfinger once and for all, thereby freeing future generations from her attacks. It was in the fall when the Cherokee would go into the forests to burn the underbrush, which allowed them to get to the chestnuts. They knew the fires would lure Spearfinger because she followed their fall harvest traditions to be near more children for her own harvest of more livers. What she didn't know is that the Cherokee had dug a gigantic pit and covered it with straw. Sure enough, she walked the path as a sweet old woman that night, singing her tune, looking for children, but she fell into the pit. She was mad, and the madder she became, her shape changed to her old stony self. The men tried to strike her with their weapons, but the spears broke off against her hard body. Some attempted to pierce her with arrows, but they just bounced off too. It was a losing battle. She started to hit rocks together to build herself a way out of the pit. Legend has it that more than one brave man fell into the hole, only to be torn apart in shreds. She finally got out, and the people thought all was lost. A great battle ensued, but she was stronger than any of them. A little bird, a tufted titmouse, appeared and sang a song to the men telling them to aim at her heart. They did, but Spearfinger just laughed. Her laughter sounded like great thunder as she kept on killing the warriors. Some of the warriors caught the bird and called him a liar and cut his tongue.

That is why the tufted titmouse has a very short tongue today.

The war against Spearfinger kept on and on. Then another bird, a Chickadee, appeared. The fearless Chickadee flew down and went underneath the old woman's right hand and flew upward, causing Spearfinger's arm to rise up towards the sky. The bird sang a song telling the men to shoot her in the heart, but the Chickadee's song informed them Spearfinger's heart was in the palm of her hand. The warriors shot arrows into her heart, and she collapsed. She fell so hard that her stone body crumbled and cemented themselves as she became a part of the mountain. The bridge she had built crumbled too and those rocks can still be seen today where they rest below Whiteside Mountain. As you walk along the jagged edges, you may see flies swarming around some of the lichen-covered ancient rocks. The flies are a warning to beware of Spearfinger.

When Brinda finished telling the tale, Arnetta was scared stiff. "Why would parents tell kids a story like that?"

"I don't know, maybe to keep the children from straying from their villages. Maybe to warn them not to talk with strangers or listen to their false stories, even though the strangers make them seem real."

"Well, it sure would have worked on me! Geez! My goosebumps have goosebumps! Thank you, Brinda."

"Thanks? Thanks for what?"

"Thanks for not telling me that while we were in the middle of the woods. All alone in the middle of the woods."

The girls talked on until well past midnight. *I guess we're not that much different from each other. Brinda seems like an old soul in a teenager's body, wise beyond her years. I know she's got a lot more experience than me. I don't know what kind of experience, but I'd like to find out. There's something about her that is so different than me, but the same somehow too. I've always felt like I'm older inside than other girls my age. It's not that I feel like I'm smarter than them or anything, it's more like I'm trapped in a sixteen-year-old body, but I don't belong here. It's like nobody understands me, so why bother. Brinda is the first person I've met that makes me feel like she's the same as me. I think we could tell each other anything.*

24

The White House

The next morning came earlier than Arnetta, and Brinda thought it would. They were both a little on edge but tried to put it past them. They dressed quickly but paid attention to every detail. After checking out of the motel, they put their bags in the car and headed to The White House. Arnetta still couldn't believe they were doing this, but there really was no other choice. She probably could've done it alone, but she was glad things had turned out as they did, and Brinda was with her. Especially since Brinda had the mirror.

They drove down the city streets of Washington. *I had no idea there was so much going on in Washington. I'm glad I picked up all the brochures from in front of the motel. I'll have to read more about them, especially the new Vietnam Memorial Wall, the Lincoln Memorial, and The Smithsonian. I've heard of The Smithsonian Institute, but I thought it was just a large building that housed artifacts, like any other museum. According to the brochure, The Smithsonian has several different buildings on the National Mall, a section be-*

tween the Capitol and the Lincoln Memorial. I never pictured Washington as being so big. When I get back home, I'll show Gummy the brochures and tell her all about the places the class went. She'll never have to know it was only a class of two.

They could see the White House, but couldn't figure out a place to park, finally deciding on a parking spot near Hotel Washington. The girls had a brief discussion about what to leave in the car, especially the mirror; it was too valuable to leave behind. Arnetta took her small purse of out her backpack and slung it over her shoulder before placing the backpack in the trunk. Brinda decided to carry her backpack but removed everything out of it except the mirror and her wallet. On the short walk to The White House, they commented on how much smaller it looked than it did in the movies. It was a humongous building, nonetheless.

Arnetta stopped on the sidewalk in front of the White House, looked around, and said, "Wow! I can't believe the most powerful man in the country lives and works there, right in the middle of all this. I mean, I didn't expect it to be like a castle with a moat or anything, and it's huge, but it's just here, sitting on this grassy lawn surrounded by a black fence."

There was a line forming at the door for a tour, so they joined in at the rear. After about thirty minutes, they were allowed inside. There was a security guard at the door. He told Brinda she couldn't go inside with her backpack.

"Here," Brinda took it off and started to hold it up for the guard, "Take a look..."

The guard put his hand on his gun. *It's like he thinks Brinda is going to try to take over The White House with the mirror or something. To give credit where credit is due, of course, the security guard had no idea what was inside the bag.* After the initial commotion, the guard confirmed there was nothing inside but a mirror and wallet. Brinda was still told her she'd have to leave the backpack at the security station until the tour ended.

"Look, Miss, you have to go out the same way you came in." he held up Brinda's bag with two fingers like it smelled bad, "This will be here when you go out. Just take the tour and come back by here when you're finished."

Arnetta tugged on Brinda's sleeve as a signal to let it go. Brinda turned and gave her a look of resignation as she placed her backpack in a big box along with personal items left by other tourists.

There really wasn't that much to see on the self-guided tour. *Not sure what I expected, but I thought we'd be seeing more than walking through a few rooms. They're beautiful, and it seems like practically every inch is clean, polished, and decorated, but I guess I thought we'd see more of the insides.*

"This is just for tourists," Brinda muttered, "The real White House is probably only seen by just a few people," then louder, "I'm going to go find the restroom."

CHAPTER TWENTY-FOUR

"Oh, OK," Arnetta added with a snicker, "Don't get lost."

Brinda looked back over her shoulder to Arnetta, rolled her eyes, and shook her head.

Arnetta shuffled along with the rest of the tour, admiring the fireplaces, bookshelves, tables, paintings, and all the things she had only seen in pictures and books. She thought she heard something, and glanced around for a brief second, then back to the roped-off section she was admiring. *There it is again.* She turned around again and spotted Brinda standing in a hallway by a thick floor-length velvet curtain. Brinda used her eyes and a quick flick of her head as a signal for Arnetta to follow. Arnetta answered Brinda with an *'are you crazy'* expression and added a small shake of her head. Brinda returned the same look, except with a nod. Arnetta fell out of the line as casually as she could but felt her knees wobble a little. *Brinda, you're going to get us arrested!* Brinda was pretending to be captivated by a life-size portrait of a lady. Then she moved on to the next painting, and the ones after that. As they wandered down the hall of artwork, the tour seemed further away, and the corridor was quiet; until it wasn't. Arnetta whispered, "Uh, oh." There were four identically suited men walking straight towards them.

"Hey, you can't be here. How did you get on this hallway?"

Brinda spoke for both of them, which was nice because Arnetta stood frozen as if she were being turned into a pillar of salt like Lot's wife did in The Bible.

"Oh, it's OK," Brinda was saying, "We're on the tour. I had to go to the bathroom and somehow got separated. We saw these paintings, and I guess you can say we got lost in their beauty. We're actually trying to find our way back; we figured this hallway loops back around?"

Man, she's good. Arnetta unconsciously slid her forearm behind her and crossed her fingers, hoping the Secret Service agents couldn't use his superhero powers to read their minds enough to know they were lying.

"I'll have someone escort you back to the tour." He grabbed at Brinda's shoulder a little too harsh as if she were going to try to make a run for it.

We're doomed. Brinda's eyes darted wildly, *I bet she probably would try to make a run for it if she could figure out where 'it' is.*

"Ouch! Leave me alone!" Brinda was not using her inside voice, and it got louder, "You're hurting me, Stop!"

Arnetta, still pretty much frozen, staring in disbelief at Brinda. *He can't really be hurting her, he's hardly touching her, more like guiding her.* Footsteps were coming from down the hall. Lots of footsteps. *Great. Now we're really in trouble. They heard Brinda, and they're sending more men in suits to take care of us.* But the wall of men opened up like the Red Sea and out from the middle, stood President Ronald Reagan! He used his right hand to let the men know to step back.

"Well, hello, ladies. What's the commotion here?"

The agent let go of Brinda's arm, and although the tension was still there, Arnetta felt a calm come over her. She looked at Brinda, who was giving her a 'go ahead' nod. She swallowed, knowing everyone noticed the large gulp, and then she looked back to the President and spoke with just a little tremble, "Mr. President, Sir, we have something to tell you about the space program that is a matter of life and death."

He looked up at the expressionless men, standing there like statues, and then to Arnetta, "Well. I wish I had time to hear about it, but I'm on my way to a meeting right now. Why don't you girls come back another time?" He started to turn away.

Arnetta touched his coat sleeve, "But, Mr. President, you don't understand. We won't take up much of your time, we promise. You have to hear us out. Please?" She dropped her hand but never took her eyes from his.

The president lowered his head in thought a couple of seconds, and then addressed Arnetta and Brinda, "Tell you what. If you can tell me why you think it's so important to talk to me right now, this very minute, I'll give you two minutes." He motioned for the secret service to step back a few feet. "Give me some space, please fellas. I'll be just a minute...or two."

Arnetta spoke while Brinda stood and nodded, "Mr. President. I've just recently come across something that I can't go into in detail about right now, but the...this thing allows you to see things." Pausing to look at Brinda with a 'he's going to think I'm crazy' look, she continued, "You see, Sir, we have the ability to see the future..."

Brinda butted in, "Sir, what she's trying to say is this. Before we even heard about that schoolteacher, Christia McAuliffe, being the first civilian to go into outer space, a friend of ours saw," Brinda made quote symbols with her fingers, "There will be an explosion shortly after takeoff. There are no survivors."

The President shot a quick glance toward the Secret Service men, and then returned his now serious face toward the girls. "Now, girls, you're stepping into dangerous territory."

"We know, Sir, what are you going to do about it?" Arnetta asked.

"No, I mean, this is a serious mess you could be in. Do you understand what you're saying? Do you know that in some instances, what you're saying could be perceived as a threat to national security?

Brinda spoke up, "Sir, we're not joking. This isn't a prank. Yes, we know this is serious, but we're not the ones to blame. We don't know anything about the how-and-why of the explosion, only that our friend saw it blow up."

"And your friend, where is she?"

"It's not a she, Sir. And he's in the hospital. He had a heart attack after he saw the explosion."

"You say he saw an explosion, but girls, obviously, The Challenger isn't even ready to go yet, so what you're basing this on is a dream? Or at best, a premonition?"

One of the Secret Service men walked up, "Mr. President, we need to get you in place, Sir."

"Oh, OK. I know."

President. Reagan turned to Brinda and Arnetta, "I'll tell you what, girls, I don't usually do this. As a matter of fact, I've never done this." He reached in his pocket and pulled out a card with his name on it and pulled a pen from his inner breast pocket. He jotted something down and handed the card to Arnetta. "Here's my number. You will be allowed to use this number only one time. Only one time, you understand? After that, the number will be disabled. Only call this number if it's an emergency. I have to go now." And just like that, the President of the United States of America walked away as the Secret Service fell into formation as a presidential shield.

Brinda and Arnetta were escorted back to the lobby by another set of Secret Service agents. It's not like they couldn't find the way on their own. *Thanks, Brinda, now*

I *feel like a criminal. Wait, what if they're taking us to the Looney bin? What if they are taking us to jail?* Arnetta found herself looking around for possible escape routes. *There are enough corridors. I could make a run for it, what are they going to do? Shoot me?* She looked at Brinda. *I don't know what she's thinking, but I can tell her mind is racing too.* Before long, they were back at the front entrance.

Brinda stopped short, almost causing the black-suited shadow to run into her. She gave him one of her watch *where you're going looks,* and then took a few steps to the security station checkpoint. After identifying the backpack, it was handed to her, and she slid it over a shoulder. Brinda took two steps and then looked at Arnetta and whispered, "Something ain't right." Before Arnetta could reply, Brinda turned, slid the backpack off her shoulder and set it on the polished mahogany table. She unlatched the buckle, flipped the flap over, and investigated the bag. The only thing inside was her wallet.

"Where is it?" she said to no one in particular.

"Miss, is there a problem?" the security person asked.

Brinda made a point of leaning forward to look at his name tag, but instead of addressing him by it, she continued, "Well, yes, there is a problem, Mr. Security Guard. You're not the same person that was here when we came through, but I gave him this backpack to keep while we went on the tour."

"Yes? Again, is there a problem?" the clean-shaven secu-rity person's face showed no expression.

"Yes, there's a problem! That's why I came back. When I left it with you, I only had two things in here," she opened up the bag for him to look inside, but he kept looking at her, "There was a wallet and a mirror in here. As you can see, if you'd look, the wallet is there, but that's all."

"Miss, I'm sorry," he stepped aside and pointed to a typed sign behind him. Large font encased lettering, in du-rable plastic, and read aloud, "We're not responsible for personal items left behind," he turned back to the girls, "Are you sure you had the...I'm sorry, did you say mirror?"

Both girls nodded. Brinda added, "Yes, sir, a handheld mirror."

"Look, I'm sorry. I don't know what to tell you. We can leave a note for the other security officers to see if they know anything about a lost mirror. You can check back with us tomorrow. Don't worry, it may show up."

A small line was starting to form behind them. Other people were waiting to pick up their belongings and some of them overheard the conversation and appeared to be more than a little anxious about getting what was theirs.

Arnetta spoke up, "No, sir, I'm afraid that won't do. You see, we're not from here, and we've got to get back on the road today. We can't wait until tomorrow. I'm sure if you just call the person that was here this morning, he could tell you what happened to the mirror, or possibly even bring it back."

"Now Miss, you shouldn't be accusing someone here of taking anything. Like I said, your belongings will probably show up when the tours are over. When the tours are over, everything is cleared from this area. Now, please step aside so the others can collect their things, you're causing a backup."

Brinda and Arnetta walked outside, but they didn't start back towards their car. They plopped down on a park bench about fifteen yards from the entrance.

"Arnetta, I'm not going back without the mirror. You can, if you want to, but I'm not going. We didn't come all the way to Washington, DC, just to lose what we came here for."

"But, Brinda, what do you want me to do? We can go back to the motel and stay another night. I think between us both, we have enough for another night. It's not that big of a deal if we don't stop to eat on the way home. We'll just eat crackers or something."

"You could call the President."

Arnetta sprang up off the bench as if she'd been stung. "What? Are you crazy?"

"You heard him. He said if you have an emergency. This is an emergency."

"Brinda, I've barely had that number for ten minutes, and you're ready to give it up already? Really?"

"OK. I see your point." Brinda shuffled her feet back and forth. "But picture this. Mr. Security Guard's curiosity got the best of him. He probably was thinking he had a nice trinket for his girlfriend, wife, or who knows, maybe he's got a little girl. Anyway, let's say he took it out. You know just to look at it. Let's say he saw a vision. I know everyone doesn't have the power of sight, but let's just say he does. If he saw something in that mirror, he might have been thinking about ways for him to profit from what he saw."

"Hmmm. Like the pot calling the kettle black, huh Brinda. I guess you would know all about the subject of someone taking the mirror for the personal gain."

"It's not like that, Arnetta, and I already told you all that. My mother needs to be able to see the mirror. She needs to believe. I know she won't take my word for it. She needs to see that her life means something, that her future has a purpose." Brinda stood, faced Arnetta, and continued, "So you see, this mirror is an emergency. It really is a matter of life and death. For my mom, for those people shooting off into space, and whatever that guard could be planning, it really could be a matter of national security!"

"Sorry, Brinda. It's just that as much as I want to get the mirror back and believe me, I do; it's just that I've been thinking about it. I've been thinking about it a lot, and that mirror? It wasn't ours to lose, Brinda. I believe that mirror picks and chooses who sees what, you know what I mean? Who knows? That man may see something that will help him."

What do you mean, Arnetta? Sure it was ours to lose! We had it in our possession, and you know what they say, don't you? Possession is nine-tenths of the law. So? Call him, Arnetta. Please? I'll never ask you to do another thing, ever again."

After a brief, but intent staring contest, Arnetta was pulling the folded-up card from her pants pocket. She gave an audible 'Argghhh,' and with a little stamp of her foot, she stormed off to the nearest phone booth. Brinda followed her to listen in and caught the end of the one-sided conversation.

"Yes, sir, I know. I'm sorry. No sir, this isn't the kind of an emergency I'd thought it would be either, but please, if you can just locate the man that was at the security check-in this morning, I'm sure this can be fixed. Yes, sir. I know. Yes sir, I will. Yes sir. I'm at the phone booth, um, oh yeah, I see the number, that's right, that's it. How did you know? Oh, never mind. Thank you. I'll wait right here for your phone call."

Brinda stepped closer. "What are you doing? Did it work? Is he getting the man to bring the mirror back?"

"He told me to wait here. He's going to call me back, or probably not him, but someone will. He also told me to lose the number because that was my only one call. It doesn't matter anyway because he said the number wouldn't work anymore anyway. I can hold onto a get-out-of-jail-free-card playing Monopoly longer than I just held the phone number to the President of the United States. Unbelievable."

They both jumped when the shrill ring sounded. Arnetta answered immediately. "Hello? Yes. OK. I see. I'm sure it was. Thank you, sir. That means a lot to me. To us. Yes sir. I know you do. Thanks again." Arnetta hung up the phone. Even after talking to the President in person less than an hour ago, it was just dawning on her she'd had three conversations with the President of the United States of America, which is probably why she just looked at Brinda. She saw Brinda's mouth moving but wasn't quite hearing her.

"Well? Earth to Arnetta. What'd he say?"

Arnetta reported the conversation as best she could, "They found the mirror. The security officer will bring it to us here in just a few minutes. It was all a misunderstanding and the man that took it apologized. He's also not a security officer anymore."

"That's great, Arnetta! Thanks."

"Wait, that's not all."

"What do you mean?"

"Well, he also said he had put in a quick call to NASA after talking to us this morning."

"Gee, that was fast."

"I know. Mr. Reagan said NASA assured him they were taking every precaution just like they do on every mission, and that he shouldn't worry. He then went on to say I shouldn't wor..."

"I believe this belongs to you?"

Arnetta reached out to accept the mirror from the former security officer. *Wow, that was fast.* "Yes, thank you very much! I'm sorry about...well, I'm sorry about the misunderstanding."

He nodded, turned, and walked away, leaving Brinda and Arnetta standing next to the phone booth.

Brinda turned towards Arnetta, "You got any more quarters?"

"Yeah, I think so, why?"

"I think I'll call my mother, just to say hello."

25

The Long Ride Home

The girls decided to head home. There was more to see, but they'd seen enough this trip, and their mission was accomplished. Well, almost.

Standing beside their car, in front of Hotel Washington, the girls decided to put the mirror in the trunk for the long ride home. There was really no need to worry about clothing getting wrinkled, so Arnetta wrapped the mirror in her dirty clothes to help protect it. While Arnetta was pulling clothes out of the tote that had been haphazardly folded, she proceeded to wrap them around the mirror. Every time she'd pull something out, Brinda made a comment.

"Here, let me help." Or "Whadja bring that for?" or "That's a cool tie-dyed shirt, did you make it or buy it?"

"Brinda, thanks, but I can do this. I know what I'm doing. I have to pack this just right so it will fit on top of my bicycle. It's hard enough having the trunk lid hanging over my head like the sword of doom."

"Well, it looks like you brought enough for a week." Then Brinda started to rifle through the rest of Arnetta's tote. As soon as Arnetta would pull something out on one end, Brinda was picking up things and asking questions about something she got from the other end.

"Stop it." Arnetta pleaded, "I think we're making a scene. See those people over there?" Arnetta nodded her head to a couple across the street, "They're probably trying to figure out what in the world we're doing. They're liable to call the police, and I don't know about you, but I've had enough interactions with authority today."

Brinda never hesitated before she shouted towards the onlookers, "Take a picture, it'd last longer!"

Arnetta raised her head faster and higher than she intended. "Ouch!" Arnetta's hand instinctively went to her bumped head to feel for a cut, "Brinda, are you crazy? Have you lost your mind? Please just get in the car and let me do this."

"OK, but just one more. What's this Arnetta?"

Arnetta grabbed the black-and-white composition book out of Brinda's hands. "What are you doing, Brinda? Please leave my things alone! If you need to know, this is my journal, and I'm telling-not asking- you now, never, ever look inside. If you think Adam and Eve got into trouble when they disobeyed the orders of the Almighty, you ain't seen nothin' yet."

"Wow! Arnetta, I didn't know you had that in you. Ok, ok. I won't look inside your precious journal. I will respect your privacy."

"Great. Now that we've got that out of the way, can we please get a move on? Those people are giving me the creeps."

Something caught Brinda's eye once again, and before Arnetta could stop her, Brinda pulled out a Polaroid camera out of the tote. "Cool, I didn't know you had a camera, Arnetta."

"It belonged to my mother. She loved taking instant pictures with it. My dad didn't like the Polaroid at all. He used a Rollei box camera. Anyway, that one doesn't have any film."

Of course, that didn't stop Brinda from play-acting. She stepped back, looked through the viewfinder, and found the couple that had been looking at them, they were still watching. Brinda pressed the button and then scurried around to hop into the front seat and pretended to remove a freshly printed photo and blew on it. It was as if she'd captured a national secret. Arnetta watched, shook her head, and rolled her eyes. *Crazy. That girl is crazy.*

Finally satisfied everything was in a safe place, Arnetta slammed the trunk shut, walked to the driver's side, and slipped inside. Brinda was still holding the camera, looking through the viewfinder. Brinda turned the camera towards

Arnetta and pressed the button again, making a noise like an unprocessed photo was spitting out.

"What, pray tell, are you doing?" Arnetta asked, cocking her head to the side.

"Maybe I could become a photographer. I'm just testing it out."

"I don't think many photographers use a Polaroid, Brinda."

"Well, there's always a first time, isn't there? Besides, I was just thinking."

"Uh oh, that can be dangerous," Arnetta was trying to keep her smirk from being too obvious," What? What have you been thinking?"

"We should buy some film for this thing and take some pictures, so you'll have proof you've been to Washington."

"I need proof?"

"Well,...what about your grandmother? And L.M.?"

Arnetta started the car, checked and rechecked her mirrors, then pulled out onto 15th Street, then she answered with, "I guess we can get a couple of packs of film, help me look for a market," then she added, "The film isn't cheap you know. We have to plan pictures, not just waste film."

"Yes, Ma'am, aye, aye sir, and all that. You are so careful, Arnetta. Why are you always so careful? It's like you, I don't know, it's like you're afraid to live life or something.

CHAPTER TWENTY-FIVE

It's like with Craig, you don't have to treat him like he's Humpty Dumpty."

"What? What are you talking about? Humpty Dumpty? I do not treat Craig like Humpty Dumpty."

"Yeah, but when you talk about him, it's like he's a movie star, or you're afraid he's going to break. When he *saw* you in the mirror? He was smiling. I think he really likes you, but you're going to have to loosen up a bit. If you want my opinion."

"Yeah. About Craig? I haven't planned on telling him about this trip just yet, and I'm not telling him much about the mirror either, Brinda. I haven't known him that long yet, and it's just that he asked me to the dance, and he's so nice, I don't want him to wonder about my sanity if you get my drift."

"Yeah, I know. You saw yourself in a dress for the dance, and Craig saw you two dancing together. All of that was in the mirror, so why not talk about it?"

"Brinda, I'd accepted Craig's invitation before he knew anything about the mirror. He was just playing with us. He doesn't know the power of the mirror, and I'd like to keep it that way...for now. I guess it's obvious he can't see things like we do, or that afternoon could've turned out differently."

"Well, I've got to admit you had me going. I'm OK with that. I told my mom about the mirror, though, and I'd like for her to try and see if she has the gift of sight, plus, I don't think she'd believe me without proof."

Arnetta squirmed a little, keeping her eyes on the road and scanning for a place to stop. "There! Look, and just our luck, there's a parking spot right in front." As she maneuvered the car between the tight parallel lines, she added, "Brinda, I know we're all excited about the mirror, but we'll have to be careful with it too. You heard L.M."

"I know. I know, it's just that I'd love for my mom to see what I saw."

"That's just it, Brinda, there's no guarantee any of us will see the same thing as someone else. I'll run in and get the film, you get ready to load it, Miss Photographer."

Now armed with an evidence producing camera, the girls took about an hour and set out on foot to snap pictures of Arnetta in front of the Lincoln Memorial, the Vietnam War Memorial, the Capitol, and the White House as well as other places. It was more of a sprint than a sightseeing tour, but the job was now complete. The pictures and the brochures from the motel would look good in a scrapbook, but now it was time for the drive home.

The trip wouldn't take nearly as long if they'd used the interstate, but both preferred the back roads to the busier routes. Since it was already early afternoon, they stopped for some hamburgers, getting extra for a meal in the car along the way.

After an hour on the road, Brinda commented, "It always seems shorter coming back from somewhere than it does going, have you ever noticed that?

Arnetta turned to Brinda in the passenger seat, "I don't know, to me, it's a long way anyway we look at it, but it's nice to have someone to talk to."

And, they did. They talked and talked for hours. The subject of Craig came up more than once, and Brinda gave another insight, "You change when we talk about Craig, did you know that?"

"What do you mean?"

"I don't know, it's just different somehow. You sort of lighten up. That's it, your whole face brightens up when you talk about Craig."

"Does not." And then, looking towards Brinda, "Really?"

"Yes, really. Hey, next town we go through, let's stop. It's time to switch drivers, OK?"

"Sure. I could stretch my legs anyway."

They drove a bit farther, to just over the North Carolina line. Brinda pointed to a billboard for a mall in Reidsville up ahead. "There! Let's stop there."

Arnetta navigated the stop according to Brinda's direction, and they ended up right in front of the Belk entrance. "You know, we could have stopped anywhere, we didn't have to pull into the mall parking lot."

"Arnetta, if you're going to the dance with Craig, you've got to get a dress. The dance is Friday night, and I really don't think you'll have another chance to go shopping anywhere else, do you? Anyway, you might as well stretch those dancing legs and look for a dress at the same time, right? C'mon, let's go."

"I didn't bring enough money with me, Brinda. I left my dress money at home."

"Don't worry, I've got some. You can pay me back later. Come on, it'll be fun."

"They walked into the Bridal department to went directly to the formal wear. Arnetta slid the hangers across the rack, making an annoying scraping sound every time she mentally discarded one dress to look at another one.

Brinda tugged at her elbow, "How about that one?" She was pointing to a dress on a mannequin propped up against the dressing room door.

"Oh my gosh!"

"I know, isn't it pretty?" Brinda smiled, proud of her find.

"Brinda, that's it! That's *the one!*"

"I know, right? Can I pick them or what? But you have to try it on, dingleberry. I mean, it's a great color and everything, but you have to try it on to make sure it's the one."

"Brinda. Listen to me. It's the dress I saw in the mirror that afternoon at L.M.'s store. I have to get that dress.

Brinda, I don't believe this. This just happened, we didn't plan to come here, and we didn't know this dress would be here. It's just like I saw in the mirror!" *Oh, I can't wait for Craig to see this, and Gummy and Papaw. That beautiful purple dress. I can't believe I'm seeing it for real, I thought it was a made-up dream.* Arnetta looked at the price tag. "Oh no, Brinda. I was afraid of that. This dress is $150.00! I can't afford that."

"Oh Arnetta, that much? Oh no! I'm afraid my pockets aren't that deep either."

"So, you like that one?" a saleslady walked over from the next rack of clothes, "I couldn't help but overhear your conversation. It is a beautiful dress, isn't it? Too bad it got damaged."

"Damaged? Both girls chimed in unison.

"Yes, someone forced it over the mannequin's head without undoing the little clasp at the back. There's a little rip near the shoulder seam. Hardly noticeable, but we can't sell it as new anymore, and besides, we're getting ready to start putting out the new spring line next week. This one is destined for the discount rack. I was thinking fifty percent off, but come to think about it, seventy-five percent is what it should be."

"Are you kidding me?" Arnetta looked stunned. After a quick calculation, dividing the price by four, she added, "This dress? For $35.00??

The saleslady smiled, "Well, close. More like $37.50 before tax. Interested?"

"Yes, Ma'am! I'll take it! Can I try it on?

26

Stops Along The Way

The girls decided on a detour via Cherokee. It really wasn't out of the way, and they had talked about how anxious Brinda was to see her mom. Because Brinda had hope, she would try her best to make sure her mom could envision a brighter future. She would be the strength her mom needed to stay the course, and Brinda would enforce it by being there for her mom instead of running from any problems.

They rode in silence for that last half hour. Arnetta figured Brinda needed the time to get ready to see her mom, and she, herself, needed to sort a few things out as well. After reaching Cherokee, she took Brinda up on the offer to sleep in her room so she could start her trip home refreshed. By the time they arrived, it was very late; the girls decided to leave everything in the car for the night.

Brinda's home was a small, single-story home and close to other houses of the same size. All were set in a row of sorts with a few trees in the front. Even though it was dark, Arnetta supposed the back yards of the homes led to the forest because no lights were coming from houses or streetlights there. Arnetta thought again about Spearfinger. How terrifying it must have been to hear stories like that and live so close to a dense forest.

Brinda went in while Arnetta stayed in the car. A few moments went by, and then Brinda appeared in the doorway, motioning for Arnetta to come in. Once inside, Brinda made a brief whispered introduction between her mom and Arnetta with promises of catching up in the morning.

Although there wasn't much privacy in Brinda's room, because it was shared with her now sleeping siblings, both girls slept together on a pallet made from two blankets with another for cover. They were both exhausted, but there's always that few minutes the body needs to prepare for rest. Brinda chose that time to talk, again in whispers.

"Arnetta, I'd almost forgotten this, but listen to this, I'll tell you a bedtime story; my grandfather told me this story when I was little.

An old Cherokee chief told his grandson, "My son, there are two wolves inside each of us, and there is a constant battle between them. One of them is evil and shows anger, jealousy, greed, resentment, inferiority, lies, and ego. The other is good and shows joy, love, peace, hope, humility, kindness, and truth. The boy thought about what his grandfather said and asked,

Grandfather, which wolf wins? The grandfather answered. The one you feed, my son. The one you feed."

"Wow! That really is profound. Thanks, Brinda, we should all live by that."

"Yes. We should. And I guess I haven't. I let fear and resentment overshadow the good things. I shouldn't have left my mom. I guess I didn't realize she needed me as much as I needed her, even though she wasn't there for me. Tonight, I could see it in her eyes when I walked in the door. She was just sitting at the kitchen table, but when I walked in, I could already see some of the joy in her eyes, you know, the same joy I saw on her face in the mirror. "

"That's great, Brinda! I'm happy for you. I can't wait to talk with her more in the morning. She said she's an early riser and will wake me up by six o'clock if I'm not already up."

"Arnetta?"

Sleep was starting its slow descent over Arnetta as she answered, "Hmmm?"

"I've decided you're right about the mirror. It really was never ours to lose. It really doesn't belong to any one person, does it? You should keep it for now. Take it back to the What's New shop."

"Good idea. Thanks for understanding, Brinda. Goodnight. My eyes won't stay open."

"Night."

When Arnetta reached Landreth the next morning, it was just before eight o'clock. She made a quick stop and dropped the duffel bag, her new dress, and L.M.'s car at the What's New shop. She climbed on her bike and rode to the hospital. The transition from the car to the bicycle was both exhilarating and exhausting, liberating and humbling. She thought about her trip to Washington in the same way. *I can't believe I just did that, what was I thinking? I'm so glad I found Brinda so she could go with me. How we got there and back in one piece, I'll never know.* Gummy wasn't the only person she'd told a 'little white lie' to. She'd told Craig she had her license. She hadn't lied about the driving courses and mechanics class, but her 'license' was a restricted license, allowing her to drive with an adult and only during daylight hours. She knew if she hadn't fibbed to Craig, he probably wouldn't have let her drive his Bella. *And after we got inside the White House? Talking to the President? I don't think anyone will ever believe me if I told them.*

Arnetta parked her bike at the entrance and went up to L.M.'s room. She'd decided to give him the short version of the last two days. *It's even hard for me to believe all we did in two days, much less anyone else. Well, technically, two days and one night. I think I may sleep for days when I get home. I'm glad today is a teacher's workday. I'm also glad I thought ahead and told Gummy not to expect me until early Monday evening.*

She told L.M. she and Brinda personally talked with President Reagan. "Because of your vision, the President said everything would be OK. He even confirmed it with NASA." She thought L.M. looked better when she'd first walked in, but after she talked with him, he seemed even more at peace. She'd also confessed to him about the driving lesson she'd taken in Craig's Mustang, Bella, and borrowing his BMW.

L.M. told her he'd be checking out in a few days. "They want to run some more tests, to rule out surgery. You know, it would be OK if you would drive me home, but maybe it's better if Craig does the driving this time. Arnetta, I'm quite proud of you. You're ready to get your license. That should be high on your list in the next few weeks. You can use my car to take your driving test if you want. I think you can do almost anything you set your mind to doing."

Arnetta walked over, gave him a hug before leaving. "I'll check in on you again, L.M. You just get better; you're looking like yourself again. Craig and I will check on the shop, bring in your mail and stuff. Speaking of Craig..., I'm going to the dance with him Friday night. I wish you could see the dress I got, but don't worry, we'll take pictures."

L.M. smiled, "I can't wait to see them. Have fun at the dance, Arnetta, I want to hear all about it. You better get on home now, don't worry about me, I'm not going anywhere."

They repeated their goodbyes, and Arnetta made her way back to the What's New shop to retrieve the duffel and dress. After carefully rolling the dress, still in the zippered vinyl case, she made her way home.

She walked in the door to find Gummy and Papaw sitting at the lunch table.

"Hey Gummy, hey Papaw. I'm back."

"Well, hello yourself, Arnetta. Did you have lunch with your class, or do you want a sandwich? Go on and take your things and get them put away, then sit down and tell us all about your trip."

Arnetta bounded up the stairs to her room. Sliding the duffle off her shoulder, she opened it and hung the purple dress in her closet. She then carefully removed the mirror she'd wrapped in her other clothing. Placing the mirror face down on top of her dresser, she traced the raised figure with her fingers.

A tear rolled down her cheek. The enormity of last week's happenings catching up with her as if her life had suddenly put on brakes, the memories slamming into her one by one, colliding with each other as they skidded through her mind.

CHAPTER TWENTY-SIX

She wiped the tear away, turned, and walked down the stairs towards the kitchen, towards her family. She was home. It had taken a week of uncertainty and a two-day road trip to realize an eight-year journey had ended, and she was finally home.

EPILOGUE

Tuesday, January 28, 1986

Hundreds of people witnessed live from Cape Canaveral. Countless students viewed, courtesy of NASA, a live stream in their school. Millions watched the TV news replay of the space shuttle Challenger as it broke apart at 46,000 feet, just seventy-three seconds into its flight. Originally thought to be an explosion was later explained to be a giant fireball caused by a fuel tank leak. After the fuel tank collapsed, liquid oxygen and hydrogen burst into flames. Parts of The Challenger, including the crew cabin, continued the path until it reached an altitude of 65,000 feet before its descent into the Atlantic at more than 200 miles per hour when all seven members aboard were killed. It is not known if any of the members were conscious during the two minute, forty-five seconds of descent. There were no survivors.

Much like the rest of America, Arnetta watched the six o'clock news in horror. Her heart not only felt crushed, but it was more like it had been shredded. *No, No, No! They didn't listen. They said it'd be safe. There were no survivors.* After the news, she, along with Gummy and Papaw, watched President Reagan in a live broadcast from the Oval office.

For the first time in history, President Reagan postponed his scheduled January 28th State of the Union address and held a special address about The Challenger. During that address, he took a moment and spoke directly to the students that watched the events live.

"I know it's hard for us to understand, but sometimes painful things like this happen. It's all a part of the process of exploration and discovery. It's all a part of taking a chance and expanding man's horizons. The future doesn't belong to the faint-hearted, it belongs to the brave. The Challenger crew was pulling us into the future, and we'll continue to follow."

The seven crew members of The Space Shuttle Challenger were:

Ellison Onizuka

Gregory Jarvis

Judith Resnick

Michael J. Smith

Frances 'Dick' Scobee

Ronald McNair

Christia McAuliffe

Author's Notes To Reader

Thank you for taking the time to read this fictional account of a mirror with special powers. This, like other stories, came to me by asking what if. In this case, what if someone saw a future event unfolding and wanted to try to stop the event from happening. Can you think of times in your life that you wish things had worked out differently?

There have been many tragedies since January 28, 1986, some at the national level, and many closer to home, some of them may have been very personal to you, and you alone. After a tragedy or accident, you need to understand that trauma can affect your body and your mind. Talk with someone, write in a journal, and know that all things will pass. In 1985/1986, there was no internet, no social media, and no YouTube channel. It's great to have the world at your fingertips, but in some ways, it was better 'the old way.' Social media, as well as the regular newspaper, TV, and radio media, have a way of sensationalizing the story to get more listeners, hits, likes, etc. There's an old news media saying, "If it bleeds, it leads," meaning the more sensational the story, the more 'front page' attention it gets. Dwelling on any one subject can prove to be unhealthy.

An American theologian, Reinhold Niebuhr wrote a prayer in the 1930s, and since then, it has been recited by millions. It's a way to remember that we are not in control of everything, but we can choose to be brave in the things we can change, and we can also choose to let go of the things we can't. It goes like this:

God, grant me the serenity to accept the things I cannot change, Courage to change the things I can, And wisdom to know the difference.

Be sure to read Jeannie's other work

Tunnel of Time

available in

Hard Cover

Paperback

and Kindle

About The Author

Jeannie Chambers lives in a small resort town in the mountains of western North Carolina. She partners with her husband as a real estate broker and vacation rental manager, but when she looks in the mirror, she sees a mother, grandmother, dog whisperer, time traveler and much more. Her parents told her more than once, "You can go anywhere in the world you want, any time you want, just by reading a book." Her sense of direction is a little off, but she doesn't mind getting lost if it's in a good story.

Her goal is to write stories that make you think without being taught, and tickle your inquisitive bones where the only way to satisfy that itch is to read more and more. Be sure to follow her on social media and her website to catch up on her latest book news.

Twitter: @inthehighlands
Facebook: Jeannie S. Chambers
Website: JeannieChambers.com

Adobe InDesign was used for the layout

of this novel. Body text is Ghandi Serif,

Regular, 12 pt, with the main title and

chapter titles in Tangerine.